Only the Good Die Young: Crime Fiction Inspired by the Songs of Billy Joel

Edited by Josh Pachter

ISBN: 978-1-953601-43-8

Also available in ebook format.

Published by Untreed Reads, LLC
506 Kansas Street, San Francisco, CA 94107
www.untreedreads.com

ONLY THE GOOD DIE YOUNG

Crime Fiction Inspired by the Songs of Billy Joel

edited by Josh Pachter

Untreed
Reads

CONTENTS

Introduction..i

Cold Spring Harbor...1

  Why Judy Why by Robert Lopresti 3

Piano Man..17

  Piano Man by Terrie Farley Moran 19

Streetlife Serenade...29

  The Entertainer by Jenny Milchman...................... 31

Turnstiles...47

  James by Barb Goffman..49

The Stranger 65

  Only the Good Die Young by Josh Pachter......... 67

52nd Street..77

  Zanzibar by Jeff Cohen 79

Glass Houses...91

  It's Still Rock and Roll to Me by Richie Narvaez 93

The Nylon Curtain 109

  Goodnight Saigon by Richard Helms 111

An Innocent Man...125

  Easy Money by John M. Floyd................................127

The Bridge..139

  A Matter of Trust by David Dean 141

Storm Front 157

  The Downeaster 'Alexa' by Michael Bracken 159

River of Dreams..173

  No Man's Land by James D.F. Hannah...................175

Acknowledgments 189

About the Contributors..191

Introduction

As I write this introduction, it is September 29, 2020, and the world is at war against a deadly and heartless foe: COVID-19.

Because so many of us are spending so much time homebound, hoping to avoid infection, online quizzes and questionnaires have become even more popular than they already were:

Post ten images from films that influenced you without explanation.

Pick the five albums you'd take with you to a desert island.

Name the twenty best cover versions of other people's songs.

You know what I'm talking about, right? You've probably Facebooked and Snapchatted and Instagrammed your way through a bunch of these things yourself.

I tend to avoid them. Most, I figure, are posted by data miners looking for hints to my various passwords. I even scroll past those that originate with people I know, because who's got time for all that jazz, ya know what I mean? As we used to say on Long Island, where I grew up, fuhgeddaboudit.

If it was just you and me at a bar, though—remember bars?—sipping a couple of cold ones and shooting the breeze, and you asked me to identify ten films or five albums or twenty covers, sure, I'd play along.

Some of those questions would be harder than others to answer—I only get to pick *five* desert-island albums? are you fuggin' *kidding* me?!—while others would be lots easier.

Here's one of the easy ones:

What was the best concert you've ever been to?

While you're busy coming up with your own answer, let me tell you that I *love* live music, and I have been to a *lot* of shows in my day. Some acts I've seen many times (David Bromberg, Jackson Browne, Gaelic Storm, Dan Hicks, Stephen Kellogg, Bill Kirchen,

Loggins and Messina, Phoebe Snow), some only once (Jimmy Buffett, Creedence, Jefferson Airplane, Paul McCartney, Simon and Garfunkel, Cat Stevens), and some I deeply regret *never* have seen live (the Beatles, Joni Mitchell, the Stones, Warren Zevon).

If I had to pick one single favorite, though, it would have to be a show I saw on September 29, 1990, exactly thirty years ago today.

I was in what was then called West Berlin, in a country that was then called West Germany, and it was four days before what the Germans would call Unification and the rest of the world would call *Re*-Unification. I was living in the Bachelor Officers' Quarters at Templehof Air Force Base and teaching active-duty American military personnel and their college-age dependents for the University of Maryland's European Division (later renamed the University of Maryland University College and recently renamed yet again the University of Maryland Global College).

On September 29, it took me an hour to ride the S Bahn from the Templehof station all the way out to the end of the line at Pichelsberg, at the southwest corner of Olympic Park, and from there it was about a five-minute walk to the Waldbühne, the Forest Stage, an outdoor amphitheater that seats over twenty-two thousand people and was built for the 1936 Berlin Olympics on the order of Nazi propaganda minister Joseph Goebbels.

In honor of the evening's performer, I brought with me a bota bag filled with Long Island Iced Tea, and I sat on an uncomfortable concrete bench in the stands and got pleasantly buzzed until Billy Joel and his band took the stage and the music started ... at which point the thousands of us in attendance jumped to our feet and never sat down for the next three hours. I don't remember exactly what songs Billy played, but this was the *Storm Front* tour, so he surely did "The Downeaster 'Alexa'" and "We Didn't Start the Fire" and the album's title track. I assume that David Brown and Liberty DeVitto must have been on lead guitar and drums, respectively, but the person I most remember—other than Billy himself—was Crystal Tagliaferro, who was new to the band and had more energy than the rest of them combined. That woman just *tore up* the stage, and the moments when Billy let her solo were as impressive as his own pyrotechnics both vocally and on the piano.

That was one hell of a show.

And Billy Joel is one hell of an entertainer, still—three decades later—selling out Madison Square Garden multiple times a year.

*

William Martin Joel was born in the Bronx in 1949 but grew up in a Levitt home in Hicksville, out on the Island. He started piano lessons at four, was playing in bars while still in high school, cut several unsuccessful records with the Hassles in the late '60s and one as half of the duo Attila in 1970—and released his first solo album, *Cold Spring Harbor*, on the Family Productions label in 1971. It didn't sell very well, and Billy himself has never been happy with it.

More success came with his second album, *Piano Man*, released by Columbia in '73—it charted at #27 on the *Billboard 200*, and its title track went to #25 on *Billboard*'s Hot 100.

Streetlife Serenade ('74) and *Turnstiles* ('75) were a step backward commercially, but after a year without an album release in '76, 1977's *The Stranger* put Billy into the Top Ten for the first time, rocketing all the way up to the #2 slot, with the single "Just the Way You Are" winning both Record of the Year and Song of the Year at the 1979 Grammys.

In '78, *52nd Street* featured three Top 40 singles, became Billy's first #1 album, and received the Album of the Year Grammy in 1980—the only one of his twelve studio records to earn that accolade. This was not the Piano Man's last Grammy, though: he took home the Best Rock Vocal Performance, Male award for his next album, 1980's *Glass Houses*, which sat at the top of the Billboard chart for a month and a half, and was honored with the Grammy Legend Award in 1991.

Five more studio albums followed *Glass Houses*—*The Nylon Curtain* ('82), *An Innocent Man* ('83), *The Bridge* ('86), *Storm Front* ('89), and *River of Dreams* ('93)—and those records racked up their share of triumphs. But there were tragedies, too, along the way: an ongoing battle with depression, a long history of alcohol abuse, multiple divorces, an autobiography written but never released.

Billy's last album (so far) was released in 2001, and it too hit #1 on the charts ... the *classical* charts! *Fantasies & Delusions* is in fact a recording of classical pieces, composed by Billy and arranged and played by Korean-British pianist Hyung-Ki Joo.

Since then, Billy Joel has continued to play live, breaking records with almost mechanical regularity at Madison Square Garden and other venues, and there've been an assortment of live albums, greatest-hits packages, and the nowadays almost obligatory collection of oddities from the vaults (*My Lives*, 2005), but the last release of "new" Billy Joel songs was *River of Dreams*, which will celebrate its thirtieth anniversary in 2023.

Think of that: twenty-two years from *Cold Spring Harbor* to *River of Dreams*, and twenty-*eight* years from *River of Dreams* to today.

Will there ever again be new Billy Joel music for us to enjoy?

Well, Billy confirmed in a 2019 *Rolling Stone* interview that he continues to write and declined to state flat-out that he will never record again.

For now, though, what we have are a dozen classic albums (plus the one classical album)—and, still, especially if you live in New York and can afford what's happened to ticket prices, the opportunity to see and hear him play his catalogue live.

And, now, this book.

Since there are no lyrics on *Fantasies & Delusions*, it isn't represented here, and neither are the Hassles or Attila disks to which Billy contributed. What you *will* find in this volume are a dozen short crime stories, each inspired by a lyric from one of Billy's twelve studio albums. Some of the song choices (such as "Piano Man" from *Piano Man* and "It's Still Rock and Roll to Me" from *Glass Houses*) were perhaps predictable, while others (such as "Why Judy Why" from *Cold Spring Harbor* and "James" from *Turnstiles*) might take readers by surprise.

The contributors are some of the best contemporary practitioners of short crime fiction, some of whom also wrote stories for my previous music-inspired anthologies (2020's *The Beat of Black Wings: Crime Fiction Inspired by the Songs of Joni Mitchell* and this year's *The Great Filling Station Holdup: Crime Fiction Inspired by the Songs of Jimmy Buffett*), others who appear in this volume only. Many of them are—like Billy, like me—native New Yorkers.

Thanks to the contributors' generosity, a third of all royalties from the sale of this anthology will go to support the work of the Joel Foundation, which primarily makes donations to fund arts-education initiatives but in 2020 contributed more than half a million dollars to aid relief efforts in response to the coronavirus.

So pour yourself a Long Island iced tea, put an appropriate platter on the stereo, turn the page, and dig in. What follows may be crime fiction to you, but it's still rock and roll to me!

Josh Pachter
Midlothian, Virginia
September 29, 2020

Cold Spring Harbor

Released November 1971

"She's Got a Way"
"You Can Make Me Free"
"Everybody Loves You Now"
"Why Judy Why"
"Falling of the Rain"
"Turn Around"
"You Look So Good to Me"
"Tomorrow Is Today"
"Nocturne"
"Got to Begin Again"

All songs by Billy Joel.

Why Judy Why
by Robert Lopresti

"How we gonna run this?" asked Feliz.

Shaw raised an eyebrow. "You mean good cop/bad cop? Is that necessary? She already confessed, didn't she?"

Feliz had her eyes closed and her back against the gray cinderblock wall. She was doing stretches, part of her usual prep for a long interrogation.

"Yup, she started blabbing soon as Jackson rang her doorbell, but she's had time to think now. We have to expect a different attitude. And she's a celebrity, so the press will be all over this."

"Okay. I'll take bad guy. She'll expect a woman to sympathize."

Feliz shook her head. "I don't think so. Given the circumstances, I think she views women as adversaries. Let's play it that way."

"Fine. But I still think she's busting to tell."

The detectives walked into the interrogation room.

Judith Partch looked at them with no sign of emotion. *She was never a beautiful girl,* Feliz thought, *but with care and taste and money she has matured into a handsome woman.*

Close to fifty, long black hair in a braid, no hint of gray, a cream-colored business suit. The only trace of color was an oval red glass hairpin at the top of her braid. No other visible jewelry, tattoos, or distinguishing marks, unless you counted a trace of musky perfume.

Not the appearance you might expect from a famous artist. Not what you might expect from what she claimed to be, either.

As they sat down opposite her, Shaw did the introductions. "Can we get you something to drink? Water, tea, coffee?"

Judith Partch shook her head. Her eyes were wary, as if expecting a trick, or the rubber hose.

"We're recording this conversation. I know you've been read your rights and signed the form saying you don't want a lawyer, but would you please repeat that for the record?"

"I don't want a lawyer."

"And you're willing to answer questions?"

"Obviously."

"How did you meet Karl Caddington?"

Judith Partch frowned. "I hoped we could leave him out of this."

Shaw's poker face bent a little. "Yeah? How do you figure?"

A shrug. "This is about me. He's not really a part of it."

Feliz spoke for the first time. "The thing is, Judy—do you mind if I call you Judy?"

Her lips pursed. "I'd rather you didn't."

"I'll try to remember that. The thing is, juries want to hear about motive." She leaned back in her seat, as if that miserable excuse for furniture was a cozy armchair. "You and I know people hardly ever *have* motives, at least none they understand. But juries like to pretend we have reasons for what we do."

The artist scowled at her. "People have reasons."

"We do? Like what?"

"Love. Hate. Money. Revenge."

"Fear," said Shaw. "That's a big one."

"And shame," said Feliz. "So many people commit big mistakes to cover up small ones. Don't you find that, Judy?"

"I don't know what you're talking about."

"Sorry, I guess I got off track. The point I was trying to make was that it sure looks like your motive had to do with Karl Caddington. Do you call him Karly?"

"I call him Karl."

"I'll try to remember that, too. So we have to look into him. Just to make the jury happy. Okay?"

Judith Partch took a deep breath. "If I plead guilty, there won't *be* a jury, right?"

Shaw gestured *stop*. "It's way too early to talk about pleas, Ms. Partch. That's why we have to make sure we cover everything." He smiled. "You're a painter, right?"

"Obviously." Her tone was impatient.

"Well, I took enough art classes in college to know you have to prepare the canvas before you start throwing paint on it. Think of our discussion like that. Okay?"

"Fine. What do you want to know?"

"How did you meet Karl Caddington?"

"A friend of mine teaches art at Stony Brook. She invited me to speak to one of her grad classes. He was one of the students."

"And you two became involved?"

For the first time, she smiled. "In many ways. Probably not the way you mean."

"How do you think I mean?"

"Sexually. But he was interested in me as a teacher. A mentor. A sounding board. He *slept* with other people."

"And you were okay with that?" asked Feliz, throwing a little doubt into her tone.

Judith Partch shrugged. "I won't pretend I didn't want more. But I was delighted simply to be part of his life."

"What did you do for him?"

"Everything I could. It was obvious that he was going to be one of the great painters of his generation."

"Let's talk about art for a moment, okay?" said Feliz. "What do you call your style?"

She looked irritated. "I call it painting. I call it *mine*."

"Sure," said Shaw. "But what do the critics call it?"

A sigh. "Most often they call it Abstract Realism."

"Is that a thing?" asked Feliz. "It sounds like an oxymoron. Like an open secret or acting natural."

"No, I think I get it," said Shaw. "I saw one painting of yours that started with a photo of a butterfly, right? And then you put all those colors and shapes over it...."

Judith Partch made a face, as if this were painful. "That's wildly oversimplified, but, yes, I suppose you could say that."

"And what about Caddington? What do the critics call his work?"

"Maximalism." More animated now. "Karl's work is *big* art: bright colors, bold lines, clear patterns. Very in-your-face."

"I don't get it," said Feliz. "If you were in two different schools, so to speak, what could you teach him?"

"The business side. I know a lot about presentation. How to catch the eye of an agent or a buyer. How to give an interview. Things that can make all the difference in a career." Another smile. "I wanted him to be discovered while he was still young enough to enjoy it, not wait until he was a bitter old man."

"Did it work?" asked Shaw.

"It did. He had his first solo show at twenty-eight."

"So he was a star," said Feliz. "But what did *you* get out of it?"

Judith Partch shook her head. "You don't get it, do you? I suppose there's no police equivalent."

"What do you mean?"

"Well, what if you got the chance to work with the best detective in the world? Sherlock Holmes, come to life?"

"I'd like that," said Shaw.

"But you didn't settle for being a platonic art fan, did you?" asked Feliz. "We saw photos at your house in Oyster Bay that certainly suggest you were lovers."

Judith Partch grimaced. "You had no right.... Okay. We became lovers, if you have to put it that way."

"Teacher-student romance. Isn't that against the rules?"

"Not at all. I never taught him in a course. Never was in a position to grade him."

"It must have been a big deal when you started sleeping together," said Shaw. "How'd that happen?"

A muscle tightened in Judith Partch's jaw. "A woman named Sonia Nyman."

The detectives straightened. "Tell us about her."

"There's not much to say. She claimed to be an artist. A *performance* artist. Meaning she did foolish things and expected to be admired for it."

"I thought that was called being a celebrity," said Feliz.

That earned a chuckle. "You aren't wrong. Anyway, Nyman was really just a hanger-on, a vampire, clinging to people with real talent and sucking up their energy. Dragging them off to parties for days at a time when they had deadlines to meet."

"Is that what she did to Caddington?" asked Shaw.

"For a while."

"Is that why you killed her?"

"Not at all." Judith Partch looked at Feliz through slitted eyes. "I killed her because she made Karl miserable."

"How'd she do that?" asked Shaw.

"Broke up with him. God knows why Karl cared, since he could have had a dozen like her any time he wanted. But he did care, and being dumped made him miserable."

She went silent. Shaw started to speak, but Feliz touched his arm.

Half a minute passed before Judith Partch resumed. "He came to me one night, weeping. Said I was the best place to be when he was crying."

"You seem proud of that," said Feliz.

"I suppose I am. It's good to be the one reliable thing in a person's life. Don't you think?"

"Depends what they rely on you *for.*"

"You gave him a shoulder to cry on," said Shaw. "What else did you do for him?"

"Slept with him when he wanted me to." She closed her eyes and sighed. "Maybe I should be grateful to Nyman for that. But I'm not."

"Why not?" asked Feliz.

"Because she broke Karl's heart. He said he wanted to die. To *die.*" She shook her head, as if that thought was unbearable.

"So what did you do?"

"You know what I did. I killed her."

"Wow," said Shaw. "That's a hell of a leap, isn't it?"

"I don't see it that way."

"Everybody else will," said Feliz. "She gave your emo friend a case of the weepies, so you—remind me, how did you kill her?"

Judith Partch blinked. "I stabbed her with a kitchen knife. In her kitchen."

"How many times?" asked Shaw.

"I wasn't counting. I started in her abdomen and kept going until the knife got stuck in her chest." She waved a hand at the papers on the table. "Does that match your reports?"

"Perfectly," said Feliz. "How did you get in her apartment?"

"She was an artist wannabe, remember? Desperate to hang around with talented people. And I was more established than Karl. I called and said I had read about her art and happened to be in Brooklyn and wanted to talk to her."

"Like shooting fish in a barrel," said Feliz. "Or rolling off a log."

She made a face. "You have a cliché for every occasion, Detective."

"Easy as pie, Judy. How did Karl react when you told him you killed his girlfriend?"

"Ex-girlfriend. I never told him."

"And when he found out she was dead?" asked Shaw.

The artist frowned. "I'm not sure he ever did. Or that it registered. Once someone was in the past, he was through with them."

"Wow," said Feliz. "Were you afraid he would erase *you* like that some day?"

"I wasn't just a pretty face. I was useful to Karl."

"But he wanted pretty faces, too, didn't he? We hear he was quite the ladies' man."

"Another cliché. Karl is very attractive. Obviously he wanted variety."

"How many of his other girls did you kill?"

"None!" Judith Partch scowled. "Don't you get it? If they were *his* I had no reason to touch them. It was only the bitches who betrayed him, deserted him. They were the ones who deserved to die."

"And you killed them," said Shaw. "Out of jealousy?"

"Why would I be jealous? They threw away a treasure. Should I envy their mistake?"

"Then it was revenge," said Feliz.

Judith Partch banged her palm on the table. "It was *punishment!* They hurt him. Damaged the life and work of a great artist. Take Kristyn Helmut-Estrin." She sneered. "What a name. Do you know about her?"

"To tell the truth," said Shaw, "only what you told Officer Jackson. We're trying to catch up. The records say she died of an overdose of sleeping pills."

"She did, but I gave them to her. In her fifth or sixth glass of wine."

"Jesus," said Feliz. "Just because she was dating your boyfriend."

Judith Partch shook her head. "You don't understand anything."

"Explain it to us," said Shaw.

"I did it because she *dumped* Karl. Publicly! At a party. Humiliated him, a man she didn't deserve to be in the same room with."

"Seems like nobody was good enough for Karly but you," said Feliz.

"I knew you wouldn't comprehend." Her fingers flexed. "I don't suppose I can smoke in here."

"Afraid not. We're sincerely concerned about your health."

"And after Kristyn dumped Karl"—Shaw checked a page of his notes—"he came back to you, right?"

"Of course. I was the only person he could rely on."

"For comfort."

"For sex," said Feliz. "Whenever he wanted."

Judith Partch shook her head so violently her braid bounced. "He could get that in any bar with a snap of his fingers."

"What did Kristyn do when she wasn't breaking great men's hearts?"

Another sneer. "She was *trying* to be a journalist. Writing for some crappy website, showing off her ignorance about art. That's how I got to talk to her, in case you wondered."

"We were about to ask," said Shaw. "You offered to let her interview you?"

"No. She would have told her editor, and I didn't want there to be a record. I read a couple of her articles—and, God, what a painful hour that was!—and called her. I asked if I could come up and discuss them."

"And of course," said Feliz, "she couldn't resist the chance to schmooze with the famous Judy Partch."

"Obviously."

"And again, you claim Karl had no idea what you did."

"None."

"So who was your next victim?" asked Feliz. "Sorry. Who was the next cruel bitch you punished for her interference with great art?"

A glare. "I could just stop talking, you know."

"But you won't. You're having too much fun showing us how clever you are."

"Who was next, Ms. Partch?" asked Shaw.

"Wren DeVitto." She closed her eyes. "Last Wednesday."

"So we're up to the present," said Feliz. "Which reminds me: do you know how we caught you?"

Judith Partch looked startled. "I confessed."

"To Officer Jackson, yes. But why did he ring your doorbell? You don't think we had Brooklyn cops wandering randomly through the mean streets of Oyster Bay, do you?"

"All right. What led you to me?"

"Social media." Feliz shook her head. "It's the craziest thing. Did you know there are people who actually post pictures of themselves committing crimes? Burglars who proudly snap selfies in other people's homes. Thugs who video themselves beating people up and share it with the world."

"I didn't do anything like that."

"Nope. You aren't dumb. I'm just explaining why we have cops watching Twitter and Instagram and all the rest, looking for the odd confession."

Feliz leaned forward. "And one of them noticed something strange about the death of Wren DeVitto."

No response.

"A lot of commenters thought Ms. DeVitto had been hanged. Which was weird, because we know how she really died, don't we?"

"I hit her with a metal figurine." Judith Partch made a face. "An ugly thing. I'm glad it broke."

"The point is," said Feliz, "our watcher-on-the-web wanted to know how the rumor that Ms. DeVitto was hanged got started. Usually, trying to trace a story like that to its source is a fool's errand, but she thought it was worth a shot. And she found something on the memorial page the funeral home set up." She checked a note. "Somebody wrote, *It's wrong to hang someone up that way*."

"Weird thing to write on a memorial," said Shaw.

"Isn't it? And that was you, Judy."

"Judith." Her hands flexed. "My name is Judith."

"Why did you write that? About hanging her?"

"I didn't mean it literally. I meant that *she* had kept *Karl* hanging for months. Making dates with him and then cancelling." She rubbed her eyes. "Do you know what that bitch did last month? She let him plan a trip to Zanzibar, buy tickets and everything—and then she backed out at the last minute."

"A capital offense," said Feliz. "Any jury would see that."

"Do you think you're funny? Because you couldn't be more wrong."

"Too hip for the room, maybe. So when Wren broke his heart, Karl came crawling back into your bed, is that right?"

"Breadcrumbing," said Shaw.

They stared at him.

He grinned. "I've been racking my brains for that word. My son told me about it."

"Breadcrumbing?" said Feliz. "What's that?"

"My son graduated from college last year. He and three buddies share a hellhole apartment over in Bushwick. One of his roommates is hung up on this woman who's way out of his league. About once a month, usually on a Saturday morning, she'll text him and ask if he has any plans for the evening. Of course, he says no."

"Naturally," said Feliz.

"He cancels all his plans for the day and, being an optimist, for the next day, too. And what happens?"

"I can guess."

"This sexy lady goes out to a bar or whatever. If she sees someone she likes, she goes home with him. If not, she drops in on my son's roommate. Slumming."

"A booty call," said Feliz. "Doesn't seem fair, does it? Only one of the playmates is allowed to call the other. And she can bail anytime she wants. Or *he* can bail when *he* wants, right, Judy?"

"It wasn't like that."

"Of course not. Most breadcrumbers, or whatever you call them, don't go around offing their lover's discards."

"Screw it." Judith Partch folded her arms. "And screw you. I'm done talking to you idiots."

*

"Why'd she really do it?" Shaw asked.

Feliz sipped beer.

The confession had been typed and signed. Judith Partch was in a holding cell, awaiting transport to Rikers Island. The lieutenant had congratulated them on closing three murders, and now they were celebrating at the Old Shield Tavern.

"Well, you've got your choice, don't you? *She* says she did it for art's sake. To save the next Picasso, or whoever she thinks Caddington is. The great Maximalist. But I'm guessing it was love. Or lust. She wouldn't be the first woman to throw herself away on a man and convince herself it was for some noble cause."

"Hey," said Shaw. "I've been meaning to ask. You saw some of their paintings, right? His and hers?"

"Sure. And?"

"Which did you like better?"

"I thought her stuff was kinda interesting. His just looked like a kid showing off."

"That's pretty much what I thought," said Shaw. "But I figured, what do I know?"

"You're the one who took art courses."

"Yeah, but I flunked most of them."

Shaw's phone buzzed, and he answered it.

"Oh, shit," he said.

*

As soon as Judith Partch was locked in the holding cell, she looked around carefully for cameras. There were none. The cell stank of urine, disinfectant, and God knows what else.

There was a bed of sorts, a mattress on a platform attached to the wall. She settled onto it.

Given the typical efficiency of government agencies, she guessed she had a few hours before they came back for her. Good.

She eased the glass hairpin from the top of her braid. Hidden in her hair was a ceramic blade, one of many she kept in her studio for scraping paint off canvases.

She had tucked it in as soon as she had seen the policeman approaching her door.

She lay down on the mattress, facing the wall.

The symbolism made her frown. In literature and art, the act of lying down and facing a wall represented despair, a giving up on life, and she didn't feel as if that was what she was doing, though the world might interpret her actions that way.

With the blade in her right hand, she used one finger to trace the vein in her left wrist.

The first cut hurt even more than she expected.

She had had a friend in college, Megan, who used to cut herself on purpose. Such a strange illness. Megan had given her two explanations. One, it relieved pressure, like opening a valve. Two, it took her mind off her other pains—spiritual agonies, she called them—which were even worse. After the second incident, Megan was kicked out of the school and disappeared.

Blood flowed.

That wasn't so hard, was it?

She needed something to take her mind off the pain. There would be no tomorrow, so think about the past. About the first time Karl came to her bed.

He was crying as he came through the door. "Oh, Judy. What have I done? You have to help me."

Under his coat, his clothes were soaked in blood. Sonia Nyman had proved to be the treacherous bitch Judith Partch had warned him she was. He had done what he had to, had defended himself, really.

As he had done twice more, with Kristyn and Wren.

And each time he had come to her afterward, for comfort and protection.

Each time, she had gone over it with him patiently. *Did anyone see you? Did you leave anything behind?*

He was sure his fingerprints were on that figurine at Wren's place. Of course he couldn't go back himself; the poor man was shaking so hard he could barely stand. So she had gone to wipe the damned statue clean.

She had never imagined she would take such a risk for a man, for any man.

Yet look what she was doing for him now.

The cell was overheated, but she shivered.

It wouldn't be long now.

There would be no trial. With her death, they would close the books on the three murders.

Why did you do it, the idiot detectives had demanded.

Well, that was simple. Many men in her life had used her, helped her, learned from her, loved her....

But only one had needed her.

Piano Man

Released November 1973

"Travelin' Prayer"
"Piano Man"
"Ain't No Crime"
"You're My Home"
"The Ballad of Billy the Kid"
"Worse Comes to Worst"
"Stop in Nevada"
"If I Only Had the Words (To Tell You)"
"Somewhere Along the Line"
"Captain Jack"

All songs by Billy Joel.

Piano Man
by Terrie Farley Moran

I got to tell you something up front. I hate the day shift. You work the night shift at a piano bar, you can talk yourself into thinking you're at a party. It's like all these folks came in to have a few drinks 'cause they want to hang out with you. Lots of laughs, a little flirting. All in fun for the regular crowd.

Okay, okay, I get it. That's not the part of the story you want to hear.

Here's how it all went down....

*

Arnie, the day bartender, called me a little after six in the AM, knowing full well I rarely get to bed before five. For all he knew, I could have had an audition lined up. But he don't care.

He started with his usual BS: "Johnny, buddy, I need a favor, man."

"Yeah?" I waited.

"I got some stomach bug. Must be something I ate. No way I can open. Could you—could you cover me for a couple of hours?"

I said nothin'.

Heard Arnie take a deep breath, waiting not so patiently for me to answer. He was probably eyeing the babe lying next to him, trying to remember her name so he could sound sincere when she woke up and he angled for Round Two.

In my experience, Arnie never gets sick, but he frequently gets lucky.

So that's how I wound up behind the stick on a Saturday morning. One good thing: I was the guy who closed last night. Billy shut down the piano around one-thirty and the crowd thinned out pretty quick, which gave me time to get the place shipshape. Right before closing, Bernie the Pipe came in and cleaned out the beer taps, so everything poured today would have a perfect head, not too foamy, not too scarce.

The morning crowd is nothing like the night crowd. For one thing, they tend to drink beer or coffee. And of course I have to pour a few shots for those who've had a rough night. The regulars pass around copies of the *Daily News* and argue about yesterday's scores, depending on the season. Baseball, football, basketball, hockey. Tennis was a new one. Ever since that Riggs guy challenged Billie Jean King to that "Match of the Sexes" or whatever it was called, tennis has been added to the list of topics.

And don't forget the ponies. Whatever the time of year, somebody's looking for a sure thing, be it Saratoga or Santa Anita or anywhere in-between. Some guys spend hours circling the racing form before they put in a quick call to Charlie the Book.

So there I was. Kelsey, wearing his usual grungy corduroys and rumpled sweater, was through the door the second I turned the lock. His bloodshot eyes darted around the empty room as if he'd never been here before, when the truth is he's first through the front door every single time I work a day shift, and I been here four years. He shuffled along to his usual stool in the corner and sat with his back to the wall.

I stepped behind the bar, put my hand on the coffee pot and raised an eyebrow in Kelsey's direction. He shook his head, which meant he needed a beer and a ball to shake off last night. I hit the tap for the beer and poured a shot of Seagram's Seven. He lifted the shot glass with two shaking hands, hoping to get it to his mouth. I stood by, bar rag at the ready in case he didn't make it. Old pro that he is, though, he didn't spill a drop. It took about a minute for him to feel the hit, lean back, and say good morning.

Yeah, yeah, I'm getting there. I'll speed it up.

By the time the kid came in, I had four at the bar. Second through the door was Frankie Muscles, an enforcer for Georgie Q, who owns a six-table restaurant on Tenth Avenue, actually a front for his real moneymaker, which is loan sharking. Frankie sits right there on the same stool every morning. He sips coffee and turns the pages of the *Daily News* until the pay phone rings. When it does, it's Georgie, calling to let Frankie know if he's got any work to be done today.

Then another barfly, strictly a Budweiser-in-a-bottle man with a perpetual five o'clock shadow, took his usual seat next to Kelsey. I don't know his real name or where he lives, but around here they call him Ike. Seems he was a paratrooper, 82nd Airborne, thirty years ago. After a few drinks, he usually starts talking about how grateful he is to be alive thanks to the brilliant tactics of his hero, General Eisenhower. I only witnessed it once, but there are still times after all these years Ike relives a battle or a bad jump landing. I heard from Arnie that the old man once put three young guys in the emergency room when they tried to calm him down. Glad I wasn't working that day. Normally a fight like that would get a guy barred for life, but being Ike is a war hero, Sully, our manager, lets him be.

Right before the kid come in, one of my steady night owls showed up, hoisted his paunch, and grabbed a seat at the other end of the bar from Frankie. Always a wise move. He works around the corner at that realty office on Thirty-Seventh Street. The night crowd calls him Paulie Real Deal, 'cause on a busy night he works the bar as hard as I do, trying to push rentals. His line is he's got a "real deal" for any poor sap he corners. Couple of times I've had to tell him to lay off. Folks who come in here ain't looking for a new apartment. They want to drink, sing along to Billy's piano, and forget they're overpaying for a one-bedroom fourth-floor walkup.

Gotta say I never see him on weeknights, but he's here from eight 'til closing every Saturday. Now here he was on a Saturday morning, and man, when he ordered a double scotch on the rocks, it threw me to see him step up to Johnny Walker Black. Saturday nights, he spends an hour nursing a Johnny Red and water like he's waiting for the ice cubes to melt. I figure it's 'cause his wallet is usually flat.

I asked if he wanted to run a tab, but he pushed a twenty across the bar and growled "Just keep 'em coming," and knocked the first one back in a long gulp.

I set Paulie's second double in front of his waiting hand just as the kid come in.

His blond hair was way too curly for one of those David Bowie cuts. You know, that long-in-the-back thing—a mullet, that's what it's called, right? That's what he had, a mullet. His jeans were denim bellbottoms, topped by a pink shirt with lots of extra material in the sleeves and a brown leather vest. He looked like one of those kids who are sorry they missed the Sixties and want to make up for it now. Whatever he was dressed for, it wasn't hanging out at nine AM in an empty piano bar on Eighth Avenue. Still, a customer is a customer, and hey, maybe he'd be a good tipper. I notice the young ones have no clue about tipping, they either under tip or over tip. Takes them a while to get the hang of normal. I hoped this kid was an over.

He looked at the bar stools, hesitated, then aimed for the middle seat opposite the piano. He left three empty stools between him and Frankie and two on the other side between him and Paulie.

My smile was on automatic pilot when I asked what I could get him. He ordered a pinot grigio. That caught everyone's attention. I mean, who drinks wine in the morning? Mornings are for serious drinkers and coffee drinkers. There ain't no in-between.

I tossed a Rheingold coaster on the bar in front of him and was pouring white wine into a stem glass when the phone rang. Only the kid turned towards the phone. Everyone else knew Frankie would get up and answer it. Kelsey winced, his head pounding as he waited for the jingle-jangle to stop.

After a mumbled "Hiya, Boss," Frankie pulled a worn notebook from his pocket, jotted something down, and hung up. He looked determined, like a man with somewhere to go, something to do.

I was busy unloading a case of Budweiser long necks, pushing them one by one into the chopped ice in the big silver cooler under the bar. Frankie came back to his stool, pushed a deuce into the well on my side, gave me a two-fingers-to-the-eyebrow salute, and sauntered off. As soon as the door closed behind him, Kelsey leaned across the bar in the general direction of the kid and said, "Be glad you ain't on the receiving end of whatever Frankie Muscles is giving out today."

The kid made the mistake of answering, and that's how the trouble started. He nodded at Kelsey. "He looked pretty tough. Me, I don't fight, I have to protect my hands." He held them up for everyone to see, like anyone cared.

Kelsey, always a talker, came back with, "What are you, some kind of hand model? John here"—he pointed to me—"is an actor. Tried out for a hand job in a commercial once. They said his hands were too big. Ain't that right, John? Hands too big for a hand job?"

Ike guffawed and slapped Kelsey on the back, like he had told the joke of the century.

Paulie picked up his glass and wiggled it in the time-honored signal for a refill, but I pretended not to see. Two double scotches in twenty minutes is a lot of booze. I figured to slow him down.

So then the kid said, "Actually, I came in to find out when I could speak to John, and here you are. This must be my lucky day."

I stopped loading the long necks and gave him my full attention, figuring he wanted some bartender secret like which beer makes the girls feel romantic the fastest. You'd be amazed how many times I get asked that question. I paid more attention to the kid than I normally would—but, again, I was hoping to slow Paulie down.

"I heard Mr. Sullivan is thinking of putting on a pianist Wednesday nights," the kid began.

That was true, although I don't think I ever heard the word "pianist" spoken out loud before. I couldn't even speculate how the kid knew about the Wednesdays. Maybe he was Sully's nephew, family friend, something like that. Anyway, it had nothing to do with me. I kept my mouth shut and waited for more.

After a minute, he continued: "Billy, your Friday and Saturday guy, is a friend of mine. He has another gig on Wednesday nights, so here I am, ready to audition."

Paulie banged his glass on the bar, two sharp raps. "Hey, John, I'm empty here."

I put the kid on pause and poured another double that was more like a one-and-a-half. Before I could advise Paul to take it slow, the scotch was down the hatch and he was on his feet, unsteadily aiming for the men's room. I hoped his aim would be better when he got there.

The kid sat up a little straighter and extended his hand. "Roger Markham."

Shaking hands is a regular part of a bartender's job, same as lighting smokes and listening to sob stories and giving the occasional "Atta boy!" So I shook his hand, figuring his story would follow.

Once he got started, the kid, this Roger guy, went straight to it. "I really want this gig. Playing in a place like this, well, it would give me a boost professionally." He looked at me with soulful wide eyes, hoping I'd go for his pitch.

I said nothing, absently wiped my hands on the bar towel looped on my belt, waited for him to continue.

"Billy says I should play for you first. You can tell if I'd be a good match for the people who show up on piano nights. He thinks you're the best person to know if Mr. Sullivan would want to hire me."

That was enough for me. "Listen, kid—er, Roger. I'd like to help you out, but I can't read Sully's mind. I have no idea what he likes or dislikes. Me, I serve drinks. That's my job. I don't have nothing to do with hiring piano players."

Roger started to stutter, then pulled himself together. "Billy figures, if I play for you and get your honest opinion, I'll be less nervous when I play for Mr. Sullivan. Sort of like a try-out before the try-out."

I shrugged, and I guess the kid took that as a sign I was weakening.

He gave me the sad eyes again and practically begged, "Just listen to one song, any song. Tell me what you want to hear. Whatever you think the customers would like."

So I figured what the hell. "How 'bout 'Rocket Man'? That one really brings the crowd to their feet ever since the Apollo 17 went up right before last Christmas. I guess folks like to cheer those moon landings."

"No problem." The kid sat on the piano bench and ran his fingers over the keyboard. He hit a few keys here and there to get a feel for the instrument, and then he really took off.

He had an easygoing voice that seemed to pick up and drop the emotional parts of the song at will. When he finished, he added a short riff, full of low notes, and then stood up.

I surprised myself with my enthusiasm. "Not bad. I gotta say, Sully could do worse than give you a listen."

Weaving his way back from the men's room, Paulie bounced off bar stools and came to a stop just inches from the kid's face.

His voice thick from too much scotch, he poked the kid with his index finger. "Give you a listen. Yeah, they'll all give you a listen, just like they'll give me a read—but they never, never give you the job. Nope, no break for you. Or for me."

Roger leaned back, sat on a bar stool, and looked to me for help.

I tried to give him some. "Paulie, sit down, why don't you? Have one on the house."

But Paul had decided to lecture the kid, and he didn't hear a word I said.

"I spent years working on *Canyon Clouds*, the next best thing to *War and Peace*. You think I could get an agent? That took more years, and when I finally got one interested, he wanted to chop all the good stuff out of my book. My book. I dumped him and went off on my own."

"Paulie," I said.

"Johnny, the kid needs to learn. The fix is in when it comes to guys like us, nobodies. We're the world's nobodies."

"Paul, c'mon, take a seat. I'll make some fresh coffee. Should I send out for bagels?"

I was this close to walking around to their side of the bar, but I held off. In my line of work, coming out from behind the stick to settle a dispute is the classic sign a customer's about to get bounced. Paul didn't normally cause trouble, so I gave him the benefit of the doubt.

My mistake.

His ranting got wilder. "I sent out the manuscript time after time. Editor after editor trashed it. Some of them sent rejections so fast, I knew they didn't even read it. I mean even a speed-reader needs a few days to get through a hundred and fifty thousand words."

Kelsey and Ike turned away. They had no interest in Paulie's spiel.

"Those fools missed their chance to read the lyrical description that exudes throughout the first seven chapters and explodes in chapter eight, not to mention the symbolism in the first half of the novel that morphs into hedonism in the second half."

"Man, that's tough." Roger put a gentle hand on Paul's shoulder. "I get it, though. Last month, I really thought I had a gig in a class place in Chicago, and then *pfft*—just like that, it fell through."

Paul jerked his arm upward and knocked the kid's hand away. "What are you, twenty? I been trying to get published longer than you been alive, and this morning I got another rejection, from some startup out in freaking Duluth. I am out of options. Do you know what that's like, kid, to be out of options? No, you don't. At your age, you think there's a world of chances ahead of you. But there ain't. They look like chances, but they're all dead ends. You should give up now, save yourself the pain."

I was starting to think this could go sideways any second, so I yelled, "Cut it out, Paulie! Just knock it off."

With real emotion in his voice, the kid said, "I'm sorry about your book."

And that's when Paulie gave one heave-ho and pushed the kid right off his stool. The kid's head slammed into the edge of the piano, and he went utterly still, blood oozing from his nose and ears. I lunged across the bar, swinging at Paulie Real Deal with a Budweiser long neck I didn't even realize was in my hand. I bashed him just above the ear, and he crumbled.

Sometime during the melee, Ike and Kelsey disappeared.

So, Detective McIntyre, that's why you find me here alone, with two dead guys on the floor.

Now do you get why I hate working the day shift?

Streetlife Serenade

Released October 1974

"Streetlife Serenader"
"Los Angelenos"
"The Great Suburban Showdown"
"Root Beer Rag" (instrumental)
"Roberta"
"The Entertainer"
"Last of the Big Time Spenders"
"Weekend Song"
"Souvenir"
"The Mexican Connection" (instrumental)

All songs by Billy Joel.

The Entertainer
by Jenny Milchman

Mercy leaned against the wall, trying to ease the tension in her back. Her spine felt like a series of knotted roots poking up above the soil. She was standing in a closet behind the stage, or what passed for a stage, at Burt's Tavern—really more of a platform. The "tavern" part was an exaggeration, too. Burt's was a dive.

The closet was where she waited to go on, or got dressed if she didn't have enough time to go home and change between jobs. That happened a couple of times a month—Mercy wasn't in a position to turn down shifts at the assisted-living home—but it always caused problems, working both jobs back-to-back. Her kids missed her. Her mom, who watched them, got mad.

Dive or not—or maybe *because* it was a dive—Burt's lured a decent number of men who lived in the backwoods upstate New York town of Wedeskyull, those who weren't nailed down by wives, girlfriends, kids, jobs to go to in the morning. Plus a trickle of drifters and grifters, losers and deadbeats from away who wandered in, lost, parched, looking for something.

What they found were the usual bottles lined up like soldiers behind the bar, beer on tap—a handful of local brews had been added to the swill over the last few years, their prices so shocking it hurt to think of anyone spending that much on a drink—and, many nights, Mercy up on stage.

On her platform of plywood and pallets.

In the beginning, when Mercy first got the gig, she danced, as she'd been hired to do. There was still a pole thrust into the front of the stage like a spear through an animal. But Mercy hardly ever used it anymore, and the men who sat hunched at the bar or around the scattering of rickety tables didn't complain much. Occasionally a stranger would jeer, ask when he was going to see some ass. But he got shut up pretty quick by the regulars.

Who were there to hear Mercy sing.

She'd started out humming under her breath while she swung around the pole or bent over and touched her toes, long hair brushing the stage like a broom. Worked up enough courage to croon out loud, then began raising her voice, till she got loud enough that the men, silent, their eyes soldered to her exposed body, couldn't help but hear. They listened, seeming not to notice—at least they didn't object—when Mercy's moves slowed down, fewer of them, fewer, till she finally stopped dancing altogether.

Eventually the regulars, the ones who closed Burt's down every night, started to ask for songs, call out requests. They wanted tunes from long ago, from their childhoods, Mercy's throaty version of lullabies. After a while, she began to throw in some of her original compositions, "I'll Lay You Down," "You're My One and Only Baby."

Mercy had a voice like burnt honey. *Smooth with heat,* her dad used to call it, before he walked out on her and her mom. For the longest time, Mercy thought it was her singing that made her dad stick around as long as he did.

When she sang, he was home with them again.

A tap on the closet door, and Burt stuck his head inside.

"You're up," he told her. "Big crowd tonight."

Mercy straightened, her back creaking in protest. The countless times she picked something off the floor for a resident who could no longer bend down, helped aged bodies rise and walk and lower, played hell with her own younger frame.

"Yeah, right," she said.

It was too dark back here to tell if their eyes met.

"All your adoring fans," Burt said. "Word's gonna spread."

"Will it, though?" Mercy said, then pushed back the length of cloth Burt had strung up and walked out onto the stage.

*

There was going to be a problem tonight.

Mercy could tell before she even opened her mouth. Burt didn't have real lights or anything—just one beam, canted like a crone—but she could make out the faces up front. She saw a stranger sitting there and knew by the lips glistening with liquor and the wolfish gleam in his eyes that he wouldn't be satisfied with singing. Because of him, Mercy decided to open with her biggest crowd pleaser.

Slow, coming up deep from her chest, like lava. Usually she worked up to this one. It was always met with a round of cheers and whoops when the guys recognized it.

I am the entertainer / It's all I know to do....

Mercy's redo of a classic. But where the original buzzed and jangled—a whitewater river of a song, rushing along—her version seeped out slowly.

And if I never make it / I'll still sing this song to you....

The regulars, at least those Mercy could make out, set down their glasses and tipped back, relaxing in their chairs. The men at the bar turned. This song was better than any drink Burt could pour. Full of dreams lost and perished, yet hope still sprung eternal, so long as one lone voice refused to cease.

Mercy felt herself slipping, too, losing herself in her own slow chant.

I am the entertainer / Just listen to my sound /

When I finally stop singing / I'll be six feet in the ground....

"Hey, sweetheart!"

The rough voice yanked Mercy as rudely as a dog brought up short on its leash.

"How 'bout you do something with your other cheeks?"

The song cut off raggedly, a needle dragged across vinyl.

She stood there, hot beneath her light, her one fucking light because this wasn't a real venue at all, and the song she'd been singing was a cheat, illegal probably, copyright infringement or some such, despite its power to woo and lull this piss-poor group of guys.

The microphone went slick in her hand, and Mercy was surprised to feel tears well up. She was going to cry, just like Violet, her little girl. Mercy couldn't remember the last time she had cried. Usually she had a thick skin, weathered by her mother's frequent bouts of temper.

The stranger rose from his seat. He was huge, built like a rock wall.

A spark of Mercy's mother flared inside her then. She swallowed her tears, brought the mike to her lips, not sure what she was going to say but about to speak anyway, when one of the regulars got up from his chair. It fell backward to the floor.

"You're gonna want to turn back around," he told the stranger.

Burt came out from behind the bar.

The stranger's hands formed fists, and he looked around like he wasn't sure who to start with. "Hey, I just want her to dance."

The other man faced him. "Why don't you dance the fuck outta here?"

"We don't want any trouble." Burt folded his arms over his chest. "No need to settle up."

That made the stranger turn, muttering under his breath as he forged a weaving path to the door.

The other man turned back to Mercy. "Gonna finish that song for us, honey?"

*

Mercy's set officially ended at ten, not that her set *was* official, since officially she was there to dance. The guy who'd interrupted her must've seen the sign taped up in the window: "Live Girls!" Like there might be dead ones.

Calling what she did at Burt's a *set* made her feel more like a real performer, despite the one stupid light and the occasional drunk asshole shouting at her to shut up and dance. Mercy would never quit singing, though. Even after her shift ended and she was on borrowed time, her own dime, so long as the men in the bar were content to sit, mellowed by music and alcohol, she'd pretend she'd been asked for an encore and keep going. Singing was a slow drizzle of drugs in Mercy's veins. She couldn't make herself stop any more than any other kind of addict. Her kids were asleep. The only thing she would have to deal with when she got home was her mom, who threw a fit when pressed into additional hours of service. Everything made her mother mad, though. Not much help for that.

Closing time came, and Mercy finally wound down, grabbing her stuff out of the closet and stopping at the bar where Burt was washing up. He didn't meet her eyes this time, either. It wasn't as dim out here as back behind the curtain. There was enough light to see that Burt's gaze was pinned to the counter, where he swirled his rag in circles.

"Small take tonight, Merce." Burt opened the old-fashioned register with a clang and handed her a fistful of bills, damp from the washrag.

"Burt," she said. "I sang for four hours."

"You were only supposed to dance for three."

Dance.

"Still." She was studying the clump of cash. A lone five mixed in among the singles. Not one ten or twenty. "You owe me at least another fifteen bucks." She was guessing, too upset to separate each sticky dollar and count. Because this was her fault, wasn't it? Burt was light because he'd come to her defense.

He went back to the register, stuck his hand inside.

"Here," he said. He put a plastic card in her hand.

Mercy squinted. "What's this?"

"One of those WDT thingies. Still has some value on it. Should bring us up to square."

Mercy shook her head. "I thought the town stopped using these."

It had been an experiment in—what did they call it?—an alternative economy. A similar thing was being done south of here, Ithaca bucks; theirs were Wedeskyull dollars. But the old-timers wouldn't have it. *Liberal shit*, they said. *What's next, a socialist president?* Well, that had almost happened, too.

"Might could start up again," Burt said. "Election year and all. Anyway, the card's still good a lot of places. Till what's on it runs out."

Hopefully he was right, because the cash he'd given her and her paycheck from Sunrise House were both spoken for already. Rent, electric, food, a new pair of sneakers for Vic, whose toes were already poking through his last, if not for Violet, who swore hers were just rubbing. What was on this card would have to take care of anything extra.

Mercy couldn't stand around arguing anymore. Her mom would be turning up the burner on her usual bitter simmer.

*

She didn't stop for gas, even though she was low and the mechanic at Dugger's Garage said running on fumes would shorten the life of her Corolla. Back home, she moved fast, skidding on chips of gravel on the driveway, only slowing down enough to keep from banging the front door and waking the kids.

The house was dark.

"Mom?"

She walked down the hall, pushing through shadows like cobwebs.

Why were the lights all off?

Mercy was suddenly convinced she had pushed things too far. Sung one too many songs that night, stressed her chronically stressed-out mother once too often. This time, she'd gone crazy, done something bad to the kids.

No, her mother loved Victor and Violet too much to let her temper out in their direction. So she'd taken them to punish Mercy, who she didn't love half so much, and now Mercy would never see Vic or Vi again.

"Mom?" Mercy called again in a throaty whisper, her voice hoarse from singing and the backwash of tears. "Where are you?"

She headed up to the second floor. The steps sank beneath her weight, and she reached for the railing, which wobbled in her hand.

No lights upstairs, either.

She poked her head into the first bedroom, where a cone of yellow shone from an Elsa nightlight. Mercy blinked, letting her eyes adjust. Vi lay there, knees pulled up under her belly, fists curled beneath her chin, the small hump of her back rising and falling in sleep. Mercy allowed herself one last reassuring look at her daughter, then headed back along the hall, like reentering a darkened pool.

Her own room, lodged between the children's, was empty.

But in Victor's, her mother sat on the bed, Vic sprawled across her lap. Her mom looked up, eyes blazing so fiercely they almost provided illumination. There was no other source of light in the room. Victor had declared himself too old for a nightlight, throwing it at his door, shattering the bulb and globe.

"What happened?" Mercy whispered. "What's wrong?"

"It's late," her mother hissed.

Mercy's back sagged. She was aching to lie down. "I know. I'm sorry."

"He had one of his episodes."

"I'm sorry," Mercy said again. "Was it bad?"

Her mother stared at her. "When are you going to quit this business?"

"What business? You know we need the money, Mom."

"Don't try and play me, Mercy," her mother snapped. "You *like* doing it."

The skirt Mercy wore when she sang felt suddenly, shamefully tight, the edge of the WDT card in its pocket sharp enough to slice. "I don't like it. I need it."

Her mother tossed her head, contempt in the swing of her hair.

And suddenly the anger Mercy had experienced when the stranger called her out at Burt's coursed through her body. She felt like she was being electrocuted. "Remember what Dad used to say about my singing?"

Her mother stood up, dumping Victor onto the bed so abruptly his body bounced.

They both went still. Mercy waited for the screech, the wail when Victor woke up, the sound of his sister's loyal feet thumping down the hall. Mercy's mother looked frightened by what she had done. She'd slapped Mercy plenty of times, pushed her down on the floor even, but she'd never laid a hand on one of her grandchildren.

Victor rolled over with a soft snuff of breath, reaching blindly for his blanket.

Mercy's mother pushed past her, leaving the house without another word.

*

Mercy stayed on the floor next to Vic's bed that night.

Her bedroom was little bigger than a storage closet—had probably *been* one once—with a twin mattress and space for not much else. Even at the best of times, it wasn't very appealing, though some cushioning would've felt nice against her throbbing spine. But Mercy wanted to be close to her son. She knew the nightmares that could strike him like a snake from the weeds.

But Victor slept soundly, and so did Mercy, stirring only when Violet shuffled into the bathroom to pee.

*

Sunlight painted the window, warming the room.

A whole Saturday lay ahead. Mercy's day off.

She got up, pain rippling down her spine. Her back had given her trouble ever since she was a kid taking dance at school and private lessons she'd had to quit after her dad left.

She trudged into the bathroom, opened the medicine cabinet and bore down on a bottle of Aleve with her palm.

"Hi, baby," she said to Violet, who was washing her hands.

"You didn't come home, Mommy," Vi said.

The tablets formed a pasty lump in her throat as Mercy dry-swallowed. "I'm not home?" She patted the sides of her body. "Then where am I?"

Violet giggled. "Mommy! I mean you didn't come home till *late!*"

"Oh, thank goodness." Mercy let out a sigh. "I thought maybe I wasn't here at all." She reached out, snatching her little girl into a hug, and tickled Vi all over. "But I am here, right? I'm here, I'm here, I'm here."

*

Victor woke up in pretty good spirits, and Mercy led the kids downstairs, where she found enough mix to make each one a pancake. They had run out of syrup weeks ago, so she melted her last packets of Equal—snagged from Sunrise House—in warm water and drizzled it on top.

"What should we do today?" she asked, sipping a cup of unsweetened instant. The hit of caffeine and the painkillers were causing her pain to let up, and she felt her mood soar. How she loved her kids. Whatever happened, there'd always be that.

Victor and Violet exchanged careful looks.

"Play outside?" Vi asked.

Victor made a face at her, and Violet flinched.

"Can we drive to the lake?" Vic asked. "Mom, you're not dressed."

Mercy looked down at her thighs, bare beneath the hem of her tee shirt. She thought about the skirt she'd taken off last night, the WDT card in one of its pockets.

"How about Walt's Walrus?" she said.

Violet jumped out of her seat and threw her arms around her mother's waist. Even Victor stood up, hiding a smile.

Mercy patted each child's flossy head. "Just one ride down the water slide," she cautioned. "We can't afford whole-day tickets."

"Water slide, water slide, watery, watery water slide!" Violet chanted.

It struck Mercy how beautiful her daughter's voice was, a quicksilver trickle. Even Victor listened as Violet found a tune for her words, making up a song from scratch. Like mother, like daughter.

*

The needle on the gas gauge was so deep into the red, Mercy didn't dare drive out to the water park without fueling up. The station by the Northway had a mini-mart, and a faded "We Accept WDT" sign in the window.

"They make milkshakes!" Vic shouted as they pulled up. "Can I get one?"

The promise of a ride down the waterslide had stripped him of years. He sounded like a little kid again.

"Bring your sister," Mercy said, climbing out of the car. "And tell the woman inside ten bucks at number six. Use this." She handed him the plastic card.

The kids trundled off, Victor walking slow enough that Violet didn't have to hurry to catch up. Belly swelling with love, Mercy watched them through the plate-glass window until they vanished from sight.

A car swerved across the lot, mud flecking its flanks, headed for the pump behind hers. When it skidded to a stop, its front bumper kissed Mercy's rear one.

"Fuck," she muttered. Her car didn't need any more abuse.

She glanced toward the mart. Victor and Violet hadn't come out yet. "Nice, guys," Mercy muttered under her breath. "Probably didn't save me any shake, either."

When she went inside, she found them at the register, Violet clutching Victor's hand so tight, his skin was turning red. She spoke up when she saw Mercy.

"She says we don't have enough for two shakes, Mommy, just one! And Victor started to do the bad thing! I said he could have mine, but he doesn't like vanilla, only chocolate!"

Indeed, Victor was staring at the cup in his free hand like it was full of spiders.

The girl behind the counter barely looked up. "You're actually lucky. My boss says we don't even have to *take* those cards anymore. I had to reboot the system just to make it go through."

Mercy couldn't afford a second milkshake. She was already going to have to tolerate a late notice on the electric to cover the waterslide.

Victor yanked his hand out of his sister's so suddenly she winced in pain. He clawed the plastic lid from the top of the cup, drew back his arm, and hurled the contents at the girl behind the counter.

She stood there, her who-the-fuck-cares expression washed away by shake, chest heaving, fists rising, as if it might not be too late to protect herself.

The mini-mart door opened with an electronic chime, weirdly tuneless, and the guy who'd driven so recklessly across the lot came in.

*

If Victor hadn't thrown the milkshake, Mercy and the kids would've already been gone.

Further back: if the WDT card hadn't run short and Victor had gotten his chocolate shake, they wouldn't have still been in the store when the guy came in.

Or further: if Burt hadn't come up shy when he went to pay her, she wouldn't have *had* the card in the first place.

And further still: if Mercy only didn't need to sing so damn bad....

She stood there, watching the girl try to wipe her face clean but succeeding only in smearing the goop. It looked like pus, something human and sick.

"I'm sorry," she whispered. "My son—he can't always control his behavior."

The girl's eyes, ringed with white, were fixed on a spot behind Mercy.

She turned slowly to see the guy from Burt's last night.

No, it wasn't him.

This teenager wasn't old enough for a bar, even by Burt's sloppy standards.

But his face blurred before Mercy's eyes, as if it too were smeary and obscured by shake, till it *became* the face of the guy who'd told her to shut up when she was singing.

This face wore a lopsided smile, a ghastly grin with no humor to it. "Hey, babe," the kid said to the girl behind the counter. "What the fuck is going on?"

"Creed," the girl said. "You're not supposed to be here when I'm working." Then she dropped her voice, speaking urgently to Mercy. "Go. Take your kids and get out."

Mercy reached for her children's hands.

Creed shifted sideways, barring the path to the door. "I don't think so," he said. "What'd you do to my girlfriend, little man?"

Victor opened and closed his mouth without saying anything. Violet edged closer to her brother, and Mercy felt a tug of love so fierce it weakened her knees.

Creed's mouth formed a snarl. "You little fucker. I'm gonna do you worse."

Mercy pushed the kids behind her. "If you lay a hand on—"

Creed's gaze switched, sliding down her body.

Mercy knew that look. That look was why she hated dancing.

"Mom?"

"Mommy?"

"Shut the little fuckers up," Creed said, taking a step in her direction. "Maybe close their eyes if you don't want them to see."

"Creed!" The girl behind the counter began to climb over it, not taking time to come around. "You promised me you wouldn't with anybody else. You said you'd wait for me to be ready."

Creed looked at her, and his expression changed.

The girl spoke hurriedly to Mercy. "I'm sorry. My little brother acts up too sometimes. I should of made another milkshake for free."

Mercy nodded slowly.

Then she grabbed her kids and ran.

*

She heard the girl's voice in her head as the three of them raced across the lot.

I should've made another milkshake / I'm sorry /

You said you'd wait for me to be ready.

She pushed the kids into the back seat and twisted around to see Creed bending the girl over the counter, compressing her body with his weight.

"Stay here," she ordered. "Don't come out, no matter what. You hear?"

Victor wrapped his arms around Violet. They nodded.

Mercy locked the doors and went back to the mini-mart, stepping carefully over the pad so the chime wouldn't sound.

Creed had taken the girl behind a tower of delivery cartons stacked so high only his wiry curls and a blue streak in her hair were visible.

Mercy padded toward them as soundlessly as possible, hoping her sneakers wouldn't squeak. She grabbed a can of chili from one of the shelves.

Creed was growling in the girl's ear. "You got any idea how turned on I got, seeing that bitch run?"

"Creed," the girl whimpered. "You said you'd be nice the first time."

"This *is* nice." He laughed. "As nice as you're ever gonna get it."

The girl let out a scream. "No, don't! Creed, fuck, I said stop!"

Mercy raised the can, just like Victor had done with the shake. She brought it down on the knobs of Creed's spine, right where hers always hurt.

His knees buckled, and he let go of the girl.

Mercy knew how fast a man could whip around and catch her with a backhand blow, so she was prepared. When Creed turned, lethal fury in his eyes, one fist coiled to punch her, she caught him upside the jaw with the can and heard the crack of bone.

Creed went down.

Mercy stood over him, panting.

A vehicle entered the lot, engine snorting, brakes setting with a sigh. She stepped away from the boxes and saw a trucker climbing out.

The girl wiped tears and streaks of milkshake off her face. She snuck a glance at Creed, who lay on the floor, jaw jutting at an odd angle, one hand going to his back.

"You've got a customer," Mercy said.

*

Four days after the original story ran, a second headline appeared on the front page of the *Wedeskyull Weekly Record:*

Local heroine, singer/songwriter, invited to perform on *Good Morning America*

Burt taped the article in the window, replacing the sign advertising "Live Girls!"

That night, there was standing room only.

Turnstiles

Released May 1976

"Say Goodbye to Hollywood"
"Summer, Highland Falls"
"All You Wanna Do Is Dance"
"New York State of Mind"
"James"
"Prelude/Angry Young Man"
"I've Loved These Days"
"Miami 2017 (Seen the Lights Go Out on Broadway)"

All songs by Billy Joel.

James
by Barb Goffman

Even big bad rock stars can feel nostalgic. That's why I found myself wandering from my parents' backyard to the one next door, where my old pal James's family was having a reunion. At least, that's what it looked like.

Screaming kids in shorts and T-shirts were running around on the grass with water guns, enjoying an unusually warm day for late September. The smell of hot dogs, burgers, and Coppertone filled the muggy air. Discarded paper plates stained with mustard littered long folding tables. One of the plates had fallen onto the ground, and a small brown terrier with prick ears was happily licking up what looked like ketchup remains. Over in the shade of a large maple tree, members of the older generation were sitting on green-and-white webbed fold-up lawn chairs. I hadn't seen chairs like that since I graduated from high school nearly twenty years ago and left Long Island for USC, returning only occasionally for concerts and family visits. On the cement patio under an awning, women in sleeveless dresses and men in Bermuda shorts and polo shirts were standing around chatting and drinking from red plastic cups. Hoping they were filled with something good, I headed over.

"Nick, is that you?" James broke away from the group, a grin spreading across his pale face. Bags sagged below his hazel eyes and premature gray lined his temples, but he otherwise looked like the same guy I tossed the ball around with when we were kids and listened to music with when we were teens—someone I'd lost touch with too long ago. His grip was strong as he pulled me in for a hug. "I can't believe it. It's great to see you."

"You, too. Hope you don't mind me crashing your party."

"Not at all. My folks will be thrilled you're here." He let out a deep breath. "I heard about your grandmother. I'm sorry."

"Thanks."

Nana's funeral was scheduled for later this week. My band and I had been touring, but we postponed two weeks' worth of shows when Pop called four days ago and I heard Mom crying in the background. I should have been there then. I should have come home last month when Nana had her heart attack, but the doctors said she was improving, she'd be okay. And I'd chosen to believe it because I was a selfish son of a bitch.

"So I hear you bought the house," I said, glancing up at the two-story split-level covered with white aluminum siding, exactly like ours. A "Long Island special," my pop used to say.

"Got a good price, something about knowing the owners." James smiled. "It was getting to be too much work for my folks. Marcy and I did some renovations, sold our condo, and moved in. Mom and Dad relocated to a fifty-five-plus community closer to town, where the old Waldbaum's shopping center used to be. They're—"

"Nicky!"

I turned and was smothered by a hug. I was used to fans who obliterated boundaries, especially ones who reeked of rum, like this chick did—but I hadn't expected it here. I eased her away. *Marcy?*

I should have realized it was her when she called me "Nicky." It had been her pet name for me in high school, back when she was my girl and we strolled the beach at night hand in hand before making out in the sand. Before she and James got together. She was still tall and trim. But her shoulder-length blond hair used to be dark brown. Her eyes were gleaming, and her clothes were upscale. She could easily fit in back in LA, where I now called a glass house overlooking the Pacific Ocean home.

"I can't believe it's you," she said. "We were in Fort Lauderdale last year, not fifteen miles from where you were playing. I was dying to go"—she glared at James—"but it didn't work out."

"Sorry," James said. "Your music is just a little—"

"Loud?" I supplied.

He laughed. "Yeah, that's it. You want something to eat? Drink?"

"Beer?"

"You got it."

He ambled off, and I chatted with several of his family members who were excited to see "the local boy who'd made good." Marcy hung on my arm the whole time, like she was claiming me. When James returned, I took the chance to escape, asking him to show me the renovations inside.

They'd knocked down some of the walls, giving the house a contemporary open-concept feel, with nice leather furniture and deep-pile carpets, which apparently were in again. We walked into a large library lined with bookshelves. A clean mahogany desk, with a computer sitting front and center, gleamed like a glossy guitar.

"This is where the magic happens," James said.

"You're published? That's awesome, man. When my mom told me you became an attorney and were working with your dad like he always wanted, I figured you'd traded in your dream for his."

"No, my dream's alive. But still a little out of reach. Work keeps me busy. Marcy"—he nodded with a smile at the window looking over the backyard, where she was refilling her cup with what looked like more rum than Coke—"well, she has expensive taste. But I try to write thirty minutes a day. I've written two crime novels since college, but they haven't sold."

Two novels in fifteen years? He must have seen the surprise on my face, because he said, "Marcy takes up a lot of my time."

Ah, yes, I remembered that about her.

"Anyway, I love writing—always did, you know—but my novels are missing that special something. I just can't come up with a great idea that'll make me stand out."

"You will, man. I have faith in you."

"Thanks. It might take till we're old and gray—"

"I think we're halfway there."

"Right? How'd that happen? But one day … one day I'm going to write my masterpiece." He half-laughed. "Remember how I used to talk about that? I was going to write a fucking masterpiece." He sighed quietly, but the sound reverberated through the room, echoes of disappointed dreams. "But you, you have really made it. Your last release went platinum?"

"The last three. It's been a sweet ride."

"Good for you." He bobbed his head. "Anyone special in your life?"

"No time for that." There'd been women here and there but no one long-term. "I put my music first. A lot of chicks don't like that."

"Creativity and family make for a hard balance. C'mon, let's go back out. I'm sure my mom is dying to feed you one of her lemon bars."

A giggling girl caught my attention as we reentered the yard.

"Who's that?" I asked. "She's not yours, is she?" The girl was lying in the grass, the brown terrier licking her face, and for a second I ached for the quiet life I'd never wanted. "She looks just like you."

"That's Ava, my sister's girl."

"Ahh. I figured Mom would've told me if you'd spawned."

He laughed. "We tried for years. I've always wanted my own. To read to. Play games with." His voice was low and wistful. "Turns out Marcy can't have kids, and the idea of adoption broke her up, so…."

He shrugged.

Damn. No kids. No published novel. And a wife who smelled like she belonged at an AA meeting. *Not that I don't enjoy refreshments*, I thought, sipping my pale ale, *but I usually don't double down until after dark.* I'd seen enough friends spiral into different kinds of addiction over the years that I rarely overindulged anymore.

"Hey, James, can you help me out?" a guy called.

"Sure thing." He clapped my arm. "Be right back."

Marcy caught my eye from a group of women at the other end of the patio, raised her cup in a toast, and tossed its contents back.

Nana always told me that opportunities come when you need 'em. I hadn't made it home in time to see her before she died, but maybe she'd brought me here for this opportunity. A chance to help two old friends.

They looked like they needed it. And maybe I did, too.

*

I spent the next afternoon driving around, checking out my old haunts, and arrived at the restaurant at seven. It had been my family's special-occasion destination when I was a kid. Pricey menu. Right on the water. In high school, my friends and I used to rag on the rich "city people" who flocked here and to other spots like it—the guys who wore sports jackets in the heat and the women with tits so fake they really could work as a shelf. The people who *summered* on Long Island's East End. Now I realized they were the people who kept the area's economy going, giving a lot of the locals enough money to live on through the winter season. Considering the size of my bank account, these days the locals probably considered *me* one of the city people.

I wandered out to the deck and spotted Marcy sitting at the corner table I'd requested—reserved under her name for privacy. Its big blue umbrella matched the sparkling Atlantic Ocean behind her. Seagulls wheeled under puffy clouds dotting the pink-and-orange sky. A picture-perfect sunset.

Marcy rose as I reached the table, and I pecked her cheek. A sweet fragrance tickled my nose, reminiscent of the perfume she'd worn in high school. I took a chair facing the water.

"Thanks for coming." I hadn't explained why I'd invited her and James to dinner—and why I'd asked her to arrive a half hour early, alone.

"Of course." She leaned forward and squeezed my hand, her engagement ring catching the light. The diamond was much smaller than the ones I tended to see, but classy, like James. "It's been too long, Nicky." A waiter arrived with a bottle of white wine. "I took the liberty."

That, unfortunately, was no surprise.

"To old friends," Marcy said, after the waiter poured two glasses and left us.

"Old friends."

We clinked our glasses, and she took a large sip.

"I heard you'll be playing at the Garden this winter. I don't drive in to the city very often. The traffic around here is terrible, much worse than when we were kids. But maybe I'll make an exception, if you can get me tickets ... and a back-stage pass."

"Sure." I leaned forward, and she did, too. "How are you, Marcy?"

"I'm good. Now." She slid her finger down the side of her glass, drawing a bead of condensation.

"You working these days?"

"I make jewelry that I sell online. And I'm part-time at the gift shop at the yacht club. Just something to keep busy. Lots of interesting people there."

"Really? I thought you wanted to be a teacher."

She laughed. "Yeah. Back in high school, getting out in the middle of the afternoon and having the summers off sounded pretty good, especially teaching first or second grade, since there'd be no tests or homework to mark up. But it wasn't for me."

"Why not?"

"Turns out little kids aren't the best conversationalists. They run around and yell and don't listen. After two years, I'd had enough." She finished, then refilled her glass.

The waiter returned. "Can I interest you in our specials? We have a lovely sea bass in a sweet chili teriyaki sauce served with shiitake sticky rice. And a scrumptious fluke in a lemon butter sauce, caught just this morning."

"They sound delicious," I said. "But we're expecting someone, so we'll have to wait."

"Would you like an appetizer in the meanwhile? We have a wonderful ahi tuna tartare, also fresh from the sea."

Damn, I loved living by the ocean, whether here or out west. I shifted my attention to Marcy to see what she thought. She was staring at me like *I* was the catch of the day.

"Maybe in a little while," she told the waiter, her eyes never leaving me. "But feel free to bring another bottle of wine when we finish this one."

We'd downed more than half of it already—or, rather, she had.

"Yes, ma'am." He stepped away.

"Look, Marcy." I tried to find the right words. "I know it's been a lot of years, and I'm sorry if I'm overstepping, but we used to be close once, so ... it's okay to open up to me ... about anything."

She tilted her head, confused.

"You don't have to pretend. I know you and James can't have kids."

"He told you that?"

"Yeah. It must be hard to live with those spare bedrooms and no kids to fill 'em."

She hesitated. "Is that how you feel? About kids?"

I thought about James's niece, how she'd tugged at my heart. I could have another life. I certainly had enough money now. I could give up touring, just live in LA and record. Find someone to love. Do the stay-at-home-dad thing like John Lennon once did. Of course the band wouldn't like that. Frankly, neither would I.

"No. Kids are fine for other people. But they don't fit into my life."

She nodded. "Well, you're right. I can't have kids. It was hard to accept at first, but I've adjusted."

She finished her glass and reached for the wine bottle. I covered her soft hand with my own. "Why don't you let me catch up?"

Marcy leaned back in her chair and slowly slid one leg over the other, reminding me of Sharon Stone in *Basic Instinct*. "Okay. Tell me about LA. Is it as wonderful as I hear? Do you live in Beverly Hills? Or that other place? The even more expensive one." She snapped her fingers. "Bel Air."

"No, I'm in a more low-key area. Still nice, though."

"I bet." She reached for the wine bottle again, almost like she didn't realize what she was doing, as if the bottle was a part of her body she couldn't stand to be without. "What's it like, going on tour?"

"It's everything I dreamed it would be. Jamming with great musicians in front of thousands of people who are screaming and singing along to music I wrote. Welcomed in cities across the world like royalty. Paris. Tokyo. Vienna. It's a huge high."

Her eyes twinkled, and I remembered the girl she'd been. So eager for her life to start. And then she took a big gulp of wine, reminding me why we were here. What Nana would want me to do.

"Marcy, if something's wrong, you can tell me. I want to help you."

She leaned forward again, giving me a good glimpse of her breasts as her long red nails grazed my arm. "You do?" Her words had taken on a breathy quality. "Because I can help you, too. We can help each other."

Fuck. This conversation had taken a bad turn. "No. Not like that."

She caressed my scrubby beard. "You're still single, right? That's what I read online."

I jerked away. "Yeah, but—"

"And now you've come home, and you wanted to see me alone tonight. It's okay, Nicky. I understand. I want it, too."

"No. I just wanted to talk to you."

"Dirty talk? I can do that. I can do anything you want. *Be* anything you want."

Jeez. "That's not what I had in mind. I want to help you and James."

"You can help me by taking me away from James. C'mon, Nicky. You got what you wanted. The fame and fortune. The shrieking fans. But you're missing someone to love you and take care of you. I can be that person. We had it great back in high school. We can have it again. I've never stopped loving you."

This had been such a mistake.

"You don't love me," I said. "And I don't love you. For God's sake, we broke up two decades ago. You've been with James ever since."

She exhaled loudly, exasperated. "Because I wanted to make you jealous. When you dumped me, I wanted you to realize what a mistake you'd made." Her eyes watered. "But you weren't jealous. You didn't seem to even care. And he treated me so good. And he was gonna be a lawyer, that's what his parents always said. That's why I stayed with him through college, married him right after we graduated from Stony Brook. I figured he'd eventually work at one of those big firms in Manhattan. We'd live in a fancy apartment in the city. A palace in the sky." Her anguish over her lost dreams tore at me. "But he didn't do that. He wanted to come back home and work in his dad's puny practice. So I'm stuck here, waiting for something better to come along." She swigged her wine, then clasped my hand. "We don't have to settle anymore, Nicky. I've seen the pictures in the magazines. Always one girl after another, no one permanent. I know why. You've been waiting for me. It's okay to admit it."

I gently removed her hand from mine. "No, Marcy. I'm sorry."

She stared at me, looking as shocked and miserable as she had that night in high school when I told her that my plans didn't include her. Tears slid down her cheeks. She jumped up from the table, grabbed her purse, and ran out onto the boardwalk. *Shit*. I looked around for the waiter but couldn't spot him, so I threw some cash on the table and followed her, hoping like hell no fellow diner had videoed our scene on their phone. Wouldn't TMZ love that?

Despite her high heels, Marcy moved pretty fast. It took me a couple of minutes to catch up to her. By the time I did, she'd run out onto a deserted pier and was leaning over the railing, looking out at the ocean, the waves thrashing beneath us. The sun had set, and the stars were sparkling against the inky black sky, just like the night I'd ended things nearly twenty years before. Her tears glittered that night, too.

I touched her shoulder. She twirled and threw her arms around my neck. "I knew you'd follow me."

Same old Marcy. Strong. Strategic. She'd been the one who snuck into *my* bedroom window when we were teens. The one who went after what she wanted, always. We were a lot alike in that way.

She kissed me hard. Desperately. I could taste her wine on my tongue.

"No," I said, shoving her away. "This isn't right, Marcy, for either of us. I don't know why you're unhappy, but let me help you. I'll pay for therapy. Or rehab. The best in the country. If you and James need time alone, you can hang at my beach house in Hawaii for as long as you want. I'll cover the plane tickets, if that'll help. Whatever you need."

"I don't need rehab. I need you! If you're worried I'll get pregnant, don't be. I'm on the pill. I won't interfere with your life. I wanna be part of it. Go on tour with you, everything."

"The pill? I thought you couldn't get pregnant."

She sneered. "I just told James that so he'd stop asking each month if I might be. He always looked so hopeful and eager. It was pathetic. I don't want any brats interfering with my life. Same way you don't. Why pour money into a college fund when you could spend it at five-star resorts in Fiji and St. Tropez? You'll take me there, won't you?"

"Is that why you told me you couldn't have kids? Because I don't want them?"

She shrugged. "You already thought I couldn't have 'em. It was easier than explaining. The point is we both want—and don't want—the same things. So come on, Nicky. Make my fantasies come true. And I'll make you happy, too, just like I used to."

It was fine to not want kids, but to lie about it to James? And to keep up that lie with me because she thought it would pay dividends? I stepped back and stared at her. She bit her lip seductively, trying to sway me. She was still that seventeen-year-old girl, waiting for someone else to give her a glamorous life instead of finding her own joy. I didn't know who I felt sorrier for, her or James.

"James has compromised his whole life for you. Because he loves you. He gave up his hope for children, sacrificed his dream of becoming an author."

Marcy rolled her eyes, contempt washing off her—and right onto me.

"My God. You've been lying all along, haven't you? About everything. Did you ever love him?"

She shook her head. "It's you. It's always been you."

She was lying again. Maybe she didn't realize it—I hadn't until this moment—but Marcy didn't love anybody but herself.

I remembered clearly now why I broke up with her. She'd never been satisfied with what she had. She'd always wanted more, especially attention. To be the center of my world. But I was determined to make a go of my music career, which required focus. So I'd ended things, clearing the way for James. He'd been crushing on her forever. I knew she'd lap that up.

I'd never considered that Marcy would stand in the way of James's goals, too. That she'd push him to become the man *she* wanted him to be. Maybe he could have stood up to his father and pursued his own dream. But he never could have stood up to him *and* Marcy. Once she got her claws into him, he was done for. He was too nice—too weak—to dump her like I did. I should have realized that. Now he was wasting his life, writing boring legal crap, when he should be writing a freaking bestseller. All in service to a woman who only pretended to love him.

It was all my fault. He'd been my best friend, and I'd left him to be devoured by a shark.

Marcy grasped my hand again. "C'mon, baby. What do you say?"

"No." I twisted away, the salty, humid air suddenly making my skin clammy. "I came here tonight because I thought I could help you. But what's wrong with you, Marcy, isn't something I can help. You're rotting from the inside out."

"Fuck you!" She slapped me, her eyes turning as dark as the ocean in winter. "Fine. If you don't want me, I'll find someone else who will. Eventually one of my rich yacht-club hookups will ditch his fat wife and whining brats for me. I'll finally get the life I deserve."

It was shocking to watch Marcy transform into a stranger, right before my eyes. Sadness wrapped around me like a heavy wool coat as I turned away.

"Where are you going?"

"To beg James for his forgiveness. To tell him about *all* of this."

Her laugh was so cold it raised the hair on my arms. "He won't believe you. The dope worships me. I'll tell him you came on to me. The rock star who thinks he can have anyone he wants. He'll never talk to you again."

Wow. She wasn't just selfish, like I'd thought. She had no soul.

Before I knew it, my hands were around her throat. I couldn't let James waste the rest of his life with this replica of a human being. He deserved way better. Marcy grunted and struggled as I squeezed. If only I hadn't sat beside her that first day of algebra. If I'd focused on the teacher instead of Marcy's legs. If—

Someone gripped me from behind and wrenched me off her. Marcy sputtered, and James stared at me, his mouth hanging open. The shock on his face mirrored the horror I felt in my bones. It was like waking from a nightmare. What had I done?

"Honey," Marcy croaked. "Call the cops. He tried to kill me. He—"

But she never finished her sentence. James slammed into her, knocking her backward against the railing. Her center of balance shifted, her arms flailed, and she toppled over the side.

"Marcy!" I tried to grab her but caught only her purse. It ripped away from her arm as she fell. Her head hit a piling with a *thud*, and she splashed into the dark water and sank from view.

Holy shit.

James and I stared down for a few moments, his breath coming hard. Then he leaned his shoulder against mine. "Listen carefully," he whispered. "She drank too much. You were trying to take her purse from her so she couldn't drive. She slapped you—that'll explain the mark on your face. That's when I got here. She was pounding on your chest. I yanked her off. Too hard. We both hit the railing, and she went over."

"What?"

"Nick, you've gotta focus. This is gonna be big news. Once the media learn you're here, they'll swarm. And people could be coming any minute now—you heard her scream as she fell."

I blinked. "I tried to take her keys."

"Her purse. Her keys are always in her purse."

"Right, her purse. She came at me. You tried to stop her. You both stumbled back, and she fell."

"Good." He pulled out his phone and dialed. "Help! My wife has fallen off the pier into the ocean.... No, I can't see her. She was drinking and went under. Please hurry!" He told the operator where we were and hung up.

"I can't believe this," I said, clutching Marcy's purse, the pebbled leather still warm from her touch.

James started to laugh, but it turned into sobbing. "I devoted my life to her, and then to hear her say...."

"What did you hear?"

"Everything. I saw her running out of the restaurant with you on her heels, so I followed. I was standing a few yards away the whole time, but my loving wife didn't notice me. I guess she really did have eyes only for you."

The pain in his voice broke my heart. "She never deserved you, dude. Neither did I. I broke up with her, *knowing* you'd go after her. I knew what she was like, knew she'd never let you get away. But I had no idea how empty she was inside."

"Don't blame yourself," he said. "You couldn't have predicted the future. Besides, it's not like I had no say in the matter. I could have ended things any time. I would have ... if I'd realized."

I hoped that was true. "Still, I should have warned you before you got in too deep. But I knew if she dated you, she'd be out of my hair. So I kept quiet."

"You think I didn't know what she was like? Nick, I *wanted* that. So cut yourself a break. We were kids. I forgive you for anything you *think* you did wrong. Just like I hope you'll forgive *me* for what I did back then."

"What you did? What are you talking about?"

His eyes widened like an owl's. "You really don't know. You think it was *your* idea to dump her? Who encouraged you to be ruthless about pursuing your dreams? I was your goddamn cheering section. Yeah, I wanted you to be happy, but I also wanted you to break up with her so she could be mine. I thought I could have it all, Marcy *and* my dreams. But instead, I've ended up with nothing."

"Not nothing. You have a chance now to find someone who deserves you. And you've got me. Your friend for life."

James's lower lip quivered. "Same here, buddy. It's why I couldn't let you kill her. I couldn't let you have that on your conscience. Not for me. And no way could I let her tell the cops what you did. Yeah, she was my wife, but you were the one who had my back."

He hugged me, and I blinked away tears. So much for my big-bad-rocker image.

The sound of sirens cut through the night. James peered over the railing once more. The waves were washing back and forth. No sign of Marcy. If we were lucky, her body would never be found.

"Should one of us dive in?" James said. "Make it look like we tried to save her?"

"No way. The water's too rough. I'll tell 'em you wanted to, but I held you back."

"Right." After staring into the distance for a minute, James said, "Your house in Hawaii, does that offer still stand?"

"Sure."

"I may be too distraught to live here anymore, after Marcy's terrible accident. I might want to go somewhere without any family to fawn over me. Somewhere I can write in peace."

"Whatever you need, man. It's yours."

"I think I've got that big idea I've been searching for. A story about love and betrayal, friendship and loyalty. About the lines people cross to make their dreams come true and the risks they take in the end to make amends and protect the ones they love."

"That's a book I'll buy."

"You think it'll be good?"

I smiled at him, and I knew that somewhere, Nana was smiling, too. "It will be a masterpiece."

The Stranger
Released September 1977

"Movin' Out (Anthony's Song)"
"The Stranger"
"Just the Way You Are"
"Scenes from an Italian Restaurant"
"Vienna"
"Only the Good Die Young"
"She's Always a Woman"
"Get It Right the First Time"
"Everybody Has a Dream/The Stranger"

All songs by Billy Joel.

Only the Good Die Young
by Josh Pachter

The way it's supposed to work—the way it works in fiction—is the door to my office swings open to reveal a stunning blonde in a tight-fitting dress, tears welling in her baby blues and a checkbook clutched in her perfectly manicured fingers, eager to offer me an outrageous amount of money (and perhaps, along the way, a taste of her luscious body) to track down her missing sister, or husband, or birth parents.

Ah, fiction.

The way it worked for me that day was different.

For starters, I don't have an office, not any more. I used to, but I was evicted nine months ago for nonpayment of rent. Times are tough all over.

So nowadays the occasional client calls me on my flip phone—I know, 2021 and I'm still using a Nokia flip that was new when Bill Clinton was canoodling in the Oval Office—and we meet at a Panera. (Starbuck's? No, thank you. I prefer my coffee to taste like coffee, though of course YMMV.)

Anyway, that's how it went on the day I want to tell you about.

She was already there when I arrived, hunched over a steaming cup of what I was willing to bet a dollar was hazelnut flavored and loaded with sugar.

She was not stunning, not blond, not sheathed in a form-fitting dress that accentuated Jessica Rabbit curves. From her appearance, she might have paid for her coffee with change she'd collected in a Mickey D's cup sitting cross-legged with a cardboard sign on a busy street corner.

And yet, as I looked down at her drawn features, her mousy-brown hair, her faded jeans and worn Pearl Jam T-shirt, a bell tinkled somewhere in the back of my mind. I had seen this woman before, once upon a time. But where, and when?

"Ms. Martin?" I parted grudgingly with the honorific.

"Mrs.," she said, her hands wrapped around her cup as if its warmth was the only thing keeping frostbite from setting in. A ghost of a smile flickered across her lips. "You don't recognize me, Tony, do you?"

And all at once the memories clicked into place. "Ginny?" I said, not believing it, not yet. "Ginny Amson?"

She raised her hands, palms facing me in a gesture of surrender, then swiveled them a hundred and eighty degrees and canted her head to one side in a parody of a "ta-dah!"

"It's Gin these days," she said. "Gin Martin."

And yes, I saw it now, a hint of the lively girl I'd lusted after long ago, washed out but not washed away.

Ginny Amson and I had only ever been in one class together, tenth grade, Mr. Forcier's Algebra II. Montague Forcier, who signed his name on bathroom passes the way it was pronounced: "4CA." I had barely managed to pass Algebra I, and the only way I made it through the second half of the sequence was by showing up ten minutes early for class with a couple of the other nimrods and trading dirty jokes with Monty back in his classroom's storage closet, in exchange for which he gave each of us what we used to call a gentleman's C.

Ginny was way out of my reach, a golden-haired goddess who wore demure white dresses to school, a tiny gold cross on a chain around her neck and no other jewelry, a smile that lit up every room she entered. I think she played the starring role in all of Mr. Forcier's nerds' dreams—I know that visions of her certainly danced in mine.

She dated Eddie Estrin, who quarterbacked the Hicksville Comets, for a couple of years, I remember that, but she was a good Catholic girl and wouldn't sleep with him. When he got tired of waiting and told her to put out or shut up, she dumped him. That's when he took up with Brenda Ford, who he later married and divorced.

After graduation, I went straight into the Army—the first Gulf War had just ended, and I figured the military would be safer for me than college, for which high school had left me woefully unprepared. After two years in khaki, I traded one uniform for another and went on the cops, had an undistinguished twenty-year career and was shitcanned in 2014 for using a chokehold on a kid who'd done nothing deserving more than a warning. Out of a job but with bills to pay and no marketable skills other than those accumulated from two decades in law enforcement, I went into private practice as a PI, and I was still scratching out a living as a professional snoop.

I'd lost track of Ginny long ago, not that I'd been keeping tabs on her. As I said, she was out of my league. A letter from home while I was stationed in Stuttgart casually mentioned that she'd married Howie Martin, who'd been the Comets' second string QB and had apparently come in to play on Team Ginny after Eddie Estrin got benched.

I looked down at her ring finger and noted the tarnished gold band. That and the name by which she'd introduced herself told me they were still a couple after all this time.

I sat across from her. "I remember you," I said. "You—"

"You tell me I haven't changed a bit," she cut me off, "I'll throw this coffee in your face."

I let that hang there for a long moment, then got back to my feet.

"I'm kidding," she said wearily. "Please, Anthony, don't go."

"I'm gonna grab myself a cup," I said. "I'll be right back."

*

The problem, Gin Martin explained, when I'd settled in across from her with a steaming mug of dark roast—no milk, no sugar, just coffee—was Howard, her husband.

I hate divorce cases, slinking around shooting evidence of infidelity through the grimy windows of no-tell motels off the Big LIE—which, if you're not from around these parts, is the Long Island Expressway, the lie being that there's anything even remotely "express" about it—but the sad fact is that divorce work accounts for the bulk of a PI's income these days, at least the bulk of mine.

So I sighed and sipped my coffee and said, "You think he's cheating on you?"

She laughed, and for just an instant I caught a glimpse of the sparkle that had made her one of the popular kids, once upon a time. "Christ, Tony, *look* at me. Of course he's cheating on me. Wouldn't you?"

The question rocked me. Back in the tenth grade, Algebra II, Monty Forcier made us occupy assigned desks, and the luck of the alphabet had me seated immediately behind Ginny Amson. In our overcrowded classroom, that meant I was close enough to smell her coconut shampoo and the hint of Charlie she dabbed on her wrists, and it was no wonder I had trouble focusing on linear equations and polynomials. All I could do was sit there and inhale the sweetness of her and daydream. Sooner or later it comes down to faith, right, and maybe, if I prayed for it fervently enough, why shouldn't I be the one?

That miracle never happened, of course. But if it had, if Ginny had noticed me and stopped hiding behind her virtuous stained-glass curtain and given me a chance, would I have cheated on her?

Then again, if she and I had gotten together and stayed together, would she have let herself go like this?

I shook myself back to the present and said, "So then what are we doing here? What do you need me for?"

"I don't mind him cheating on me, Tony. What I mind is I'm pretty sure he's decided to kill me."

*

It was hard to concentrate on the story Gin Martin told me—my mind kept drifting back to high school, to the scent of Ginny Amson's shampoo making it hard to concentrate on Old Man 4CA's frequency distributions and scatter plots.

But what it boiled down to was in fact a lot simpler than Algebra II.

In 1994, when Howard Martin, newly married, decided to open an auto-body shop on Jerusalem Avenue, less than half a mile north of Hicksville High, there was no way he could float a big enough bank loan to get the place up and running. But Ginny's parents had money and agreed to cosign the note if Howie made their daughter an equal partner in the enterprise. Still starry-eyed from the wedding, Howard agreed, and Martin & Martin Body & Paint opened its doors halfway through the Dot-Com Decade and thrived.

Aside from her ownership position, Ginny had nothing to do with the business. She helped decorate the office prior to the grand opening, but other than that she'd only visited the place twice: once in 2011, when she managed to coax her '95 Camaro the six blocks to the shop from where some asshole had rear-ended her while she was fully stopped at a red light on Newbridge Road, and again three weeks later when Howie brought her back to pick up the car, which his crew had beautifully restored to practically cherry condition, nicer than it had looked on the day she'd bought it, used, ten years earlier.

But now Howie had taken up with a bottle blonde half his age, Kitty Something, and apparently the bimbo was insisting he marry her. If he divorced Ginny, though, he'd either have to buy out her share of the shop or sell the place and split the proceeds with her and hope that left him with enough capital to start all over again somewhere else.

Instead, Ginny was convinced, her husband had decided to go with Plan M for Murder. She had filed for divorce herself, citing "irretrievable breakdown" of the marriage, but her parents had fronted the down payment on the post-WWII prefab house that had served as the Martins' primary residence since their nuptials, and she had no intention of moving out and ceding control of the home to Howard.

Which was where I came in. My mission, should I choose to accept it, was to prevent said murder from occurring during the six months or more it was likely to take while the legal proceedings unfolded.

The problem was there was no way to know when during that half year Howie might try to kill her, or how he might do it. The only way to guarantee her safety would be to lock her into a windowless vault with only one entrance, station me outside that solitary entry point 24/7, and prohibit her from eating or drinking anything I didn't bring her myself from sources I was confident were tamperproof.

And, even then—even if I had such an impregnable Fortress of Solitude (which I don't) and could stay awake and alert around the clock indefinitely (which I can't)—how long could she afford to pay a guardian angel? My going rate is two hundred dollars a day, plus expenses. In honor of the good old days, I told Ginny I'd give her my time for half price, but I'd still have to hire two more operatives, each of them taking an eight-hour shift and me doing the same plus figuring out how to feed her, so we were certainly looking at three Cs a day, bare minimum, and there was no way she could set aside that kind of jack out of her pin money for even two months, let alone six.

We finally settled on a compromise. I convinced her to vacate their ticky-tacky imitation Levitt home, after all, and check into the Econo Lodge on Duffy Avenue, right off the Wantagh State Parkway.

For the next almost two weeks, I showed up every morning at 9 AM with a day's worth of food for her and a thermos and sandwiches for myself, and until 9 PM I sat in a folding lawn chair planted right in front of Room 108's only door and made sure no one came or went.

From 9 PM to 9 AM, Ginny was on her own, but I boarded up her windows from the inside and installed a flange-style NOVA truck lock designed to withstand thirty thousand pounds of pull-away force on the door, with a ram bar vertical barrier that boasted a minimum yield strength of a hundred thousand pounds per square inch. There was no way anybody was getting through that baby unless she unlocked it, and she was under strict orders to do so for nobody—and I mean nobody—but me.

*

If only we could have skipped Day Thirteen, like elevators skip the thirteenth floor and go straight to fourteen.

Day Thirteen, 9 PM, I tucked Ginny in for the night, same as usual, and had her repeat her instructions back to me through the closed and truck-locked door: no opening up for nobody, no leaving the room for any reason.

I was home by 9:20, kicked off my shoes and popped open an Old Timey IPA from Great South Bay and switched on Monday Night Football. The Giants have dropped twenty-seven out of fifty-one games over the years to the otherwise hapless Browns, but they were up by a field goal deep in the second quarter by the time I hit the couch, and I was hoping tonight's game would bring my homeboys one win closer to parity.

When my phone rang, I almost let the call go to voicemail, but with a sinking feeling in the pit of my stomach I grabbed it off my beat-up coffee table and checked the little mini-screen on the front.

I flipped it open and said, "Ginny? What's—"

She cut me off before I could finish the question. "Anthony! He's here, Howard! He's pounding on the door! He says he's giving the little tramp up, he wants us to get back together. What should I—?"

On the TV, the Giants had possession, third and six at Cleveland's forty-yard line. Daniel Jones faked a handoff to Saquon Barkley and was dropping back to fire a screen pass to Darius Slayton, who was wide open.

"Do not let him in," I barked. "I'm on my way."

*

I squealed around the Exxon station at the corner of West Old Country Road and Duffy and into a parking space directly in front of Room 108. The door was standing wide open. "Oh, shit," I said, jumping out of my car. "Shit, shit, shit!"

I raced to the side of the doorway and eased my head around the jamb to peek into the room.

Ginny Martin was dressed in pale-blue sweatpants and a black Nirvana T-shirt printed with a photo of Kurt Cobain, bent forward at the waist, clutching a left-handed Fender Mustang, his long blond hair almost completely covering his face. There was a bullet hole in Kurt's forehead, and the blood that stained the front of the shirt was real, not a photo. It was Ginny's blood, and she'd been flung back onto the bed—where she lay face-up on the navy comforter, her sightless eyes staring at the ceiling—by the impact of the shot that had killed her.

Howie Martin had put on a few pounds since the last time I saw him, but he was still pretty fit for going-on-fifty, despite the multiple of six grams of extra weight he was carrying, depending on how many .380 ACP rounds he'd taken. It was impossible to say for sure, since he was spread-eagled face down on the bed, the fingers of his right hand resting against Ginny's cheek, as if caressing her face.

However many cartridges had been fired, I figured they were probably .380 ACPs, because the weapon the girl standing over Howie and Ginny was holding was a Smith & Wesson Bodyguard 380. A good handgun for a woman: semi-automatic, ultra-lightweight, easily concealable, a slim grip width that makes it comfortable for small hands, simple to control and aim, with a 9.5-pound trigger pull weight that makes it tough to fire accidentally.

The girl's back was to me, and the nimbus of golden curls that ringed her head concealed her face from view. She was wearing a lavender babydoll shirtdress with a gathered empire waist over floral net tights the same matte black as the gun in her extended right hand.

She must have heard me in the doorway, because without turning her head she began to talk. It was more of a mumble, really, but I could make out the words.

"He was going to leave me," she said, her voice dull and as lifeless as the bodies on the bed. "He was going back to her. I couldn't—I couldn't just let him go. I couldn't!"

I took three steps into the room and wrestled the pistol from Kitty's grasp. She struggled mightily, but she was just a wisp of a thing and her resistance was futile against my greater strength. I held her thin wrists behind her back with one hand, and with the other fished a zip-tie from my pocket and cuffed her. Gin Martin had told me she was half Howie's age, but Howard and Ginny and I were all in our late forties and if Kitty was out of her teens I'm a Martian.

Once I had her hogtied, the language that spat out of that girl's mouth would have made a sailor blush, but I wasn't listening. I dialed 9-1-1 and reported the double murder.

As we waited for the sirens, I stood there with the zip-cuffs clenched in my fist and looked down at the bodies of my long-ago classmates.

A fragment of an old song echoed inside my head.

Only the good die young.

Bullshit.

This pretty little Kitty was young, and she was not dead, but she had broken up a marriage and murdered two people in cold blood.

I wasn't sure if Howie was good or bad or somewhere in-between—I mean, I knew he'd been cheating on his wife, but that was pretty much all I knew.

Poor Gin Martin, though. Age had withered her and custom staled her infinite variety—I may not have been any great shakes in Algebra II, but I remembered my Great Shakespeare class, remembered that line from Antony and Cleopatra. Though the years had not been kind to her, she seemed to me from our re-acquaintance to have been, in all the ways that really mattered, a basically good woman.

Good enough, at any rate, to trust that Howie had meant it when he'd showed up at her motel door, pleading for another chance to make their marriage work, good enough to take him at his word and let him in, despite her promise to me to keep that goddamn door locked.

And there she lay, dead for a ducat.

Only the good die young, yeah, sure.

But sometimes the good die older, and the young live on.

God*damn* it.

Goddamn it all the way to hell.

52nd Street

Released October 1978

"Big Shot"
"Honesty"
"My Life"
"Zanzibar"
"Stiletto"
"Rosalinda's Eyes"
"Half a Mile Away"
"Until the Night"
"52nd Street"

All songs by Billy Joel.

Zanzibar
by Jeff Cohen

May 24, 1976

Muhammad Ali wasn't what he'd been, but Richard Dunn wasn't really anything, and the fight was over in five rounds. Ali danced and bobbed and got himself into a sweat, but you could tell he was holding Dunn up until *he* decided it was time to end it. Meanwhile, I had the Yanks on the radio, and they scored five times against the hapless Brewers in the bottom of the first.

But I wasn't especially concerned about any of that. There was a dead man on the floor of the bar, and I was the bartender. Not a good combination.

We'd advertised our showing of the fight because it was early in the season for us and the owners figured Ali's name, even at this late stage of his career, would bring people in. On a Monday night in Asbury Park, we could usually count on a "crowd" of maybe ten, but tonight we'd gotten sixty-two at the door. They'd each paid a handsome twenty-five bucks to see the fight and were drinking enough to keep the place going until the weather heated up and we started seeing tourists wondering if Bruce Springsteen might drop in for a surprise set. Alas, Zanzibar was about the only local place The Boss *hadn't* frequented before becoming a household name and a New Jersey deity.

I sighed. It had all been going so well before someone decided to stab the poor bastard on the floor.

For the record, I didn't see the actual stabbing; I was busy trying to figure out what a Harvey Wallbanger might be for some leisure-suited dope trying to impress his date. (It turned out the drink is basically a Screwdriver with some Galliano floating on top, but I didn't find that out until later. And the girl left alone after the cops came.)

I jumped over the bar when I heard the scream. A crowd had amassed around the center of what's usually the bandstand but tonight was the stage. A big screen had been hung from the ceiling, and a projection TV was showing the fight. But it was over, and the jukebox was playing. Billy Joel, "All You Wanna Do Is Dance," from his brand-new album.

I pushed a few customers out of the way and found the guy on the floor. I recognized him; I'd carded him on his way in because he looked to be about sixteen. But his driver's license, which looked real, said he was born in September of 1957, making him eighteen and legal.

And now he was dying from a bleeding wound in his gut—no, two wounds, small ones, distinct and deep—but I didn't see the knife or any other weapon.

"Call an ambulance!" I yelled, then realized the only phone was behind the bar and pointed at it. "Right there!"

A college girl in a Rutgers T-shirt ran to do as I'd asked.

I knelt down to try to calm the kid, but I knew he didn't have a chance.

"I didn't do nothing," he said, and those were his last words.

Eighteen. He was probably right.

The crowd still hovered over me, maybe out of curiosity or to say they'd been there when the kid cashed in, but it figured one of *them* had killed him.

"What happened?" I said to no one in particular.

The bunch of them—fight fans, college kids, a few high-school seniors, two gum-chewing women in their sixties—stared at me like third graders whose teacher had just asked them to explain quantum physics.

"What *happened*?" I shouted, and this skinny kid I recognized because he'd asked me what the cheapest beer was took a step forward.

"I think that guy got stabbed," he said.

*

Two uniformed cops arrived maybe five minutes later.

Most people—including most cops—think bartenders have some strange jurisdictional power over the saloons they work for. I hate to disappoint you, but we don't. Bouncers do, but we don't have a bouncer at Zanzibar.

The two uniforms determined the kid on the floor was dead and called for an ambulance. They told everybody to stay put and stay quiet, told *me* to stop serving drinks because the detectives would want the witnesses sober. Like they were sober when it happened.

Detective Lawrence Freeman walked in a couple of minutes later, looking like someone had rousted him out of bed, where he'd not necessarily been sleeping. His tie was loose around his neck, barely making contact with the collar of his limp white shirt. He identified himself by giving me the privilege of looking at his badge.

This was clearly not Freeman's first homicide.

"What happened?" he asked me. An overflow crowd, and he came to me first. The one person everybody could agree *hadn't* stabbed the kid on the floor.

"I didn't see it," I said. "I heard the kid yell, and he was bleeding out by the time I got to him."

"Where's the knife?" Freeman asked, as if I'd given some indication I might know.

"You sure it was a knife?" I asked. "It looks like two smaller wounds."

"You guys serve food here, right? You got utensils?"

"Yeah, but tonight was a buffet, because of the fight," I said. "There are some knives out there, you can see, for people to use, but they're pretty blunt. Wouldn't make holes like that."

"You recognize the dead guy?" Freeman said.

"Not from before tonight. He came in early, around seven-thirty. I carded him, and his license showed him to be eighteen, so I let him in."

"He talk to anybody? You hear an argument, anything like that?"

I tried to think back, but it was a crowded house, and the owners prefer I concentrate on the customers buying lots of drinks. "I don't remember anything," I told Freeman. "I think he might have been hitting on the waitress, but everybody does that, so I could be thinking about someone else."

He nodded, all in a day's work. Or a night's. "What's the waitress's name?"

"Laura." I pointed across the room, to where our resident *femme fatale* was being questioned by one of the uniforms, who was paying less attention to her answers than to her cleavage. She was probably used to it.

"And you think the kid was hitting on her?"

I shrugged. "A lot of guys were. Your officer over there is, right now. She handles it."

I didn't add that she shouldn't *have* to, but the management insisted she wear the tight T-shirts and smile a lot. She had her hair piled up in accordance with mandatory New Jersey hygiene regulations, and that should have kept the wolves at bay, right? Who am I to disagree with the people who issue my paychecks?

Freeman cocked an eyebrow. "Yeah. She handles it. She got a boyfriend?"

That presented a moral dilemma. I didn't want to rat out a good kid who I was sure hadn't killed the stiff on the floor, but I couldn't truthfully say I didn't know. "She and our busboy Rob are dating, I think." I knew that to be a fact. "But he's been in and out of the kitchen the whole night."

"Was he in the kitchen when the kid hit the floor?"

"Can we stop calling him 'the kid'? You guys must have found his wallet. Who was he?"

That was my way of avoiding telling him I'd seen Rob in the seating area right before the stabbing.

Freeman looked through his notes, which were on a reporter's notebook he carried in his back pocket. "Name's Anthony Ricciardi. Apparently works in a grocery store in Spotswood. Worked. Anyways, he's got a pay stub from them in his wallet." He looked up and made eye contact. "Whoever killed him better hope his old man isn't connected, huh?" He grinned.

He didn't ask about Rob again, but I watched him walk over toward the kitchen and talk to Steve the cook, who pointed at Rob, who was standing near but not next to Laura. She looked stunned, and now that the cop was done trying (and no doubt failing) to get her phone number, she was gnawing at her index finger and watching the ambulance personnel cart poor Anthony out on a gurney.

In no time flat, the cops were gone, giving little attention to a bar fight that had gotten out of hand. They had other fish to fry. There were probably high-school kids out on the boardwalk selling loose joints, and they had to go clamp down on that action.

Call me crazy, but the one thing I couldn't banish from my brain was the idea that Anthony's mother probably didn't know her son was dead yet. She was sitting at home, watching TV, confident everything was all right, not even imagining that the next time the phone rang her life would get a lot worse forever.

There wasn't anything I could do about that. But maybe I could find out what had happened on my watch that had ended up with her son dying on a sticky barroom floor.

*

The cops had pretty much dismissed the other customers—any one of whom might have pulled a weapon on Anthony Ricciardi—as soon as they'd frisked everyone (especially the girls) and asked a couple of questions. After that, they'd concentrated on the staff, which was me, Laura, Rob, Steve, and Marty, the spare bartender who'd been hired just for the night.

I'd worked with Marty a couple of times before on what were expected to be especially busy shifts, and he wasn't a bad guy. I walked over to him and watched him polish the same square foot of bar for a good number of minutes. "You see anything?" I finally asked.

He raised his eyebrows and tilted his head. "Nah, not really. I can't figure out how nobody saw who killed that kid. If you're asking if I did it, I was all the way over here when it happened."

"I wasn't asking if you did it," I said.

"Good, because I didn't."

Marty wasn't going to be much help, but he had raised a good point: in a packed crowd, how could no one have noticed the kid get stabbed?

"I didn't think so," I said, and walked over to Rob.

Our busboy is skinny and slight, less than five-eight, with red hair and a look of suspense, like he's waiting for the next awful thing that's about to happen. "Rough night," I said. "You okay?"

"Yeah." The word was a reflex. He probably would have said the same thing if *he'd* been the one who got stabbed. The truth is, Rob is rarely okay. He usually looks scared and tense. Laura is the one thing he can count on in the world. He's twenty-three, still a kid. He borrows his old man's car to drive to work because he can't afford one of his own. The owners pay him minimum wage, and $2.20 an hour doesn't add up to much.

I figured I'd make an end run. "How are things with you and Laura?"

"Fine."

But there was an edge to his voice, and he was looking past me, not at me. His eyes narrowed angrily. He was looking at the spot where Anthony had been stabbed. I didn't think Rob had it in him, but maybe he'd become enraged when he saw Anthony trying to pick up his girlfriend. There were all sorts of sharp implements in the kitchen.

Laura—for one rare moment not in Rob's line of sight—was talking to James Hardy, one of our regulars and her ex. He used to be a frat boy at Fairleigh Ridiculous up in Madison, and once a frat boy, always a frat boy. Laura didn't look happy, and neither did James. They too were staring at the spot where the cops had not yet cleared us to mop up the blood.

"Funny that James still hangs around here," I said, pretending to be casual. "Now that you and Laura are a thing, you'd think he'd have found another bar."

Rob's face kept that cold expression. "He'll never find another bar."

"Hey, we need all the customers we can get. Remember that."

That wasn't what I was thinking, but it was what a company man would say, and Rob thought I was a company man.

"Yeah," Rob said. "I'm gonna go clean up." He went back into the kitchen, glaring over his shoulder at Laura and James. I was left standing there, looking like I had at my seventh-grade dance, scanning the room for a friendly face to talk to.

I decided my best bet was to walk over to Laura and James, whose conversation seemed more intense than usual. I mean, a guy *had* been stabbed and killed in the bar tonight, so talking about the Yankee game—they'd hung on to beat the Brewers, 5-2—would have seemed strange.

"Either of you guys see what happened?" I asked. There wasn't any reason to start with small talk, since I wasn't particularly friendly with either of them. To Laura, I was a co-worker and her superior at the bar. To James, I was the guy who served him gin and tonic during the summer months. He never came in during cold weather. That was one of the reasons Laura dumped him: who needs a boyfriend for three months out of the year?

What was interesting was that they looked at each other before either one of them looked at me.

"No," Laura said. "I mean, I heard some yelling, and I went over, and then that guy just made a sound and fell to the floor. I didn't even realize he'd been stabbed until I saw the blood on his shirt."

She didn't make eye contact the whole time she was talking. I turned to James, so he couldn't just look away from me without it being obvious.

"I was talking to the kid," he said. "About the fight, you know. He didn't know anything about boxing and was mouthing off that Ali is old and fat. I mean, maybe *now*, but you should have seen him in his prime, that's what I told him."

My eyes narrowed. "Did you argue with him?"

James waved me off. "No. It was just the usual guys-talking-about-sports thing. He didn't care that much—and, frankly, neither did I."

I don't know why—I'll never know why—but I asked, "Did he mention Laura?" I'd gotten the impression that Anthony wanted to know Laura better and wasn't being subtle about it. And James was Laura's ex.

He didn't immediately reject the idea. "He said he thought the waitress was beautiful. I wasn't going to argue with him about that." He grinned. Laura was studying the floor.

There were maybe three other people in the room besides us when Rob—making a noise somewhere between a migrating bison and a Super Bowl pass rusher—burst through the kitchen door, heading straight for James with what turned out to be a two-pronged carving fork in his upraised hand.

"Leave her *alone!*" he screamed, as Laura gasped and James put his hands over his eyes and ducked.

I stuck out my right arm, aiming for his chest—because I wanted to avoid the tines of the fork—but I missed and clotheslined him in the neck. He fell backwards and landed on his ass on the barroom floor. The fork clattered to the linoleum and stayed there. Rob put his hands to his throat, and I bent over and picked up the fork to get it out of the way.

"What happened?" Rob gasped, his voice hoarse.

I held up the fork. "This thing has two really sharp points," I said. "Would have made two holes in James, just like the ones in Anthony."

I bent over and offered him my hand. He took it, and I pulled him to his feet.

"You saw that kid hitting on Laura, and you got mad," I said. "In the crowd, you could get as close as you wanted with that thing up your sleeve, and you could have stabbed him without anybody noticing."

"He wouldn't," Laura said quietly. She put a hand on Rob's shoulder.

"He did," James said, drawing himself up to his full height and puffing out his chest. "I didn't want to get him in trouble, but I saw him come out of the kitchen and stab that guy with the fork."

"No," Rob rasped.

"I would have done something to stop him," James went on, "but it happened too fast."

Rob looked stunned and shook his head. His voice wasn't back, but it was on its way. "I didn't," he managed.

"Did you tell this to the cops?" I asked James.

"No," he said, too fast. "Like I said, I didn't want to get Rob in trouble."

"Why not? If he stole your girlfriend and killed that kid, why wouldn't you *want* to get him in trouble?" It was a gambit and not a terribly subtle one, but it was worth playing.

"I dunno," he mumbled, sounding like someone without a decent alibi. "He seems like a nice enough guy."

"If I pat you down, am I going to find another fork?" I asked.

"No! I didn't stab the kid—*he* did!"

Laura, looking devastated, shook her head. She made eye contact with me for the first time since Anthony had hit the ground. "James hid the fork up his sleeve and ditched it after," she said. "He stabbed that boy, because he was getting fresh with me. I *told* him I could handle it, but he got mad. He's been calling me for weeks, trying to get me to go out with him again. When he saw that poor boy flirting with me, he just couldn't handle it."

James's jaw dropped, but his eyes registered anger, not fear. "That's a lie," he protested.

"He picked up the fork from the buffet table, and while everyone was watching the end of the fight he just walked up and stabbed that boy," Laura went on. "I didn't know how to tell the police without them thinking I'd told him to do it, but I *swear* I didn't!" Tears formed in her eyes, and she bit her lower lip.

I looked at Rob, then James, then Laura. Then I walked over to the bar and reached for the phone. I dialed. This wasn't the first time we'd had a bar fight, and I had the number memorized.

"Who are you calling?" Laura asked.

"The cops. Detective Freeman."

"But I *didn't do it!*" James yelled.

"Tell that to him," I said. "It's his job."

*

Freeman showed up twenty minutes later and questioned everyone again. After Laura acknowledged through tears she'd held back before that she'd seen it happen, he carted James away for "further questioning," and we all knew what that meant.

By now, I was certain, Anthony Ricciardi's mother had gotten the phone call. Rob, relieved it wasn't *him* in cuffs, gave Laura a grateful smile and went back to the kitchen to finish up for the night. Freeman said we could clean the floor, and I got after that myself. I didn't have the heart to tell anybody else to do it.

Laura went over to the front window and turned off the neon sign that read OPEN.

And that was when I noticed for the first time that she had a thin red line running down the back of her neck, just a trickle. Straight from the two sharp hairpins she was using to keep in compliance with the mandatory New Jersey hygiene regulations for restaurants.

Glass Houses

Released March 1980

"You May Be Right"
"Sometimes a Fantasy"
"Don't Ask Me Why"
"It's Still Rock and Roll to Me"
"All for Leyna"
"I Don't Want to Be Alone"
"Sleeping with the Television On"
"*C'etait Toi* (You Were the One)"
"Close to the Borderline"
"Through the Long Night"

All songs by Billy Joel.

It's Still Rock and Roll to Me
by Richie Narvaez

I don't go in much for the new music. They say people's musical taste sets by their mid-thirties. My mid-thirties was a long time ago, so by now my taste must be fossilized.

My kids play the latest pop, but I barely hear what leaks out of their ear buds for the few seconds they have them out. At the Parkway Diner, the hot new hits get piped in, but when I'm there I'm only interested in my coffee and bagel and not getting stuck on the LIE. Eddie, my barber—going on twenty years now, though I don't know why I trust a barber who wears a toupee—he keeps music on all the time, Drake, Taylor Swift, Shakira, says he's trying to stay hip and young. It's just background noise while he trims me up, though. Too much bass. Four-chord loops. Doesn't stick.

Which is funny, because I used to be such a music hound back in the day. Deejayed at my college station. At home, I had a Technics SL 1200 direct-drive turntable, paired with a Marantz 2265 solid-state receiver—sixty-five watts per channel, the classic black faceplate, perfect proportions—and Acoustic Energy AE1 speakers, only as big as a shoebox but incredible sound. Every Saturday, I would take the LIRR to Manhattan and haunt the record shops in the Village, spend every dime, spare or not, on AOR, glam, New Wave, funk, disco, pop, reggae, didn't matter.

Today, all that equipment, all that vinyl, sits piled in the garage next to the spare fridge. So far, it's survived twenty-four years of the wife's annual purges. So far.

I gave up my music jones when I joined the force—and after I gave up the force, well, who's got time?

This came to mind when I had to pick Rico up and haul ass out to Massapequa. He said the job involved an upcoming musical superstar. "He's about to break big."

"What kind of music?" I said. "Can't be rock. I don't think they *make* rock superstars anymore."

"Here we go again," he said.

"C'mon, think about it. What's the last rock album you bought?"

"I listen to—"

"Hey, I know my taste is out of style. You know what my kids call the stuff I like? 'Yacht Rock.' Like I'd ever be caught dead on a yacht."

"About the assignment," he said. Rico had been with the agency longer than me, joined after he accidentally shot off two toes. He had been a good detective, dogged, serious. "Client's name is Brandon G."

"Never heard of him."

"He's what you call Internet famous."

"Famous enough to need security, I guess."

"Well, that, and someone stole his baby-blue Continental."

*

The moment we turned onto Baldwin Place, drums started beating in my head. I used to live in Levittown, slightly north of here, and this block was familiar. By the time we pulled up near a peach-colored split-level, its sidewalk littered with reporter types, I remembered who lived there.

A second later, he came out the door. Mitch Gamberini, former lead singer of the Everlasting Neanderthals—a surf ska band that had one minor local hit, "Outside Action," in '81—and my former roommate at Stony Brook. His face was the same, except there was no spiky hair above it. No hair at all, in fact.

I had loved his band's music and had tried to make them as famous as I could on my late-night deejay slots on WUSB. It wasn't just for his sake. The more popular the band got, the more of a chick magnet they became—a big plus for me. That was how I met my first wife. Which, come to think of it, may not have been such a plus, after all....

Doug and David, two guys from the agency, were already there, keeping the reporters back. Rico and I passed them, and Mitch came up to me.

"Bobby?" he said. "Bobby Lavoe? What's it been, twenty-five years?"

"More," I said. "This is Rico Dourigan. We're with Valiant Security."

"I thought you were a city cop."

"Not for six years."

"Oh. Oh, wow."

I nodded at the reporter types. "This is all for your boy?"

"Yeah. Brandon. He's going places."

"So they tell me. How you been?"

Walking inside, we barely had time to catch up when his wife popped out of a doorway.

"Oh, my god! Is that Bobby?" she said and gave me a big kiss on the lips. "Of all the people!"

"I'm sure you remember Diane?" Mitch said.

She pulled at the tab collars on my shirt. "Oh, my god, you never used to dress like this! Remember, Mitch, Bobby was a cool punk with one cheap pair of sneakers back in the day." She returned her attention to me. "You got a lot of mileage out of those."

In 1982, Diane had been a jet-black-haired groupie, munchkin-high but fierce enough to beat back all the other groupies after Mitch. The fuchsia hair and ornate glasses she wore now showed she was still a wild child at heart.

In the living room, sunk into a plush couch, was a young man, about twenty, looking retro in pink sidewinders and a bright orange pair of pants. His longish hair covered his eyes and, like too many his age, he seemed bored by the overwhelming weight of existence. I remembered the feeling well.

"This is Brandon," Mitch said.

The kid didn't budge.

His mother plopped next to him and brushed his hair with her hand. "These men are here to help you, honey," she cooed.

Still didn't budge.

Sitting in a recliner across from the kid was a man wearing a plain white tee and jeans that belonged on a younger and thinner version of himself.

"I'm Brandon's manager," the man said. British accent. Noted. "Well, producer-manager, manager-producer. Bit of both. Bo. Bo's the name," he said, abruptly standing, shoving his hand out and leaning very close to my face. "I'm glad you're here." Liquor-at-nine-in-the-morning breath. Noted. "Brandon is a proper artist, not just some pop star wannabe. He's got to be kept safe, safe as the Bank of England, if you get my meaning."

I had met many music producer-managers back in the day. The species seemed unchanged.

"Loud and clear," I told him. "You the one called the reporters?"

"Brandon was on YouTube about it this morning. Once it's on YouTube, it's all over the world, I'm afraid, for good or ill."

"Are you going to find my car?" A tired voice, barely above a whisper. It was the kid, finally speaking.

Next to me, Mitch rolled his eyes.

Diane said, "Jesus Christ, he loves that thing. Belonged to his grandfather and his father, briefly."

"The same one you used to talk about inheriting?" I asked Mitch.

He nodded. "Same one, '63 Continental convertible, baby blue."

I whistled. "So he finally let you drive it?"

"It's mine now?" the kid interrupted. "And someone took it?" He had that annoying habit of making every statement sound like a question. "That's why you're here?"

Annoying.

From what Rico had told me in the car, we were there because the record company that had just signed the kid was throwing a busload of money at *our* company. We weren't there to do investigative work, but I know when a client needs to be placated. "We'll see what we can do," I said.

From the kid: "Just go get her? She took it?"

Rico asked, "Who's her?"

"@All4Leyna? She's been bashing me on social media, threatening me for weeks? Plus, she *said* she was gonna take it?"

"Who's this?" I asked.

"A superfan," Bo the manager said. "Proper obsessed with Brandon. She'll probably make a few videos and then return the thing. Really, there's no reason to worry."

"Oh, no?" Brandon stood and, pushing his phone into my face, asked a real question. "What about this, then?"

It was a video of him sleeping, his face lit by a television. Whoever was holding the camera dangled car keys in front of the lens, and then the video stopped.

It had been uploaded the night before. The account name read "@All4Leyna."

"This looks like a police matter," I told them. "We can put you in—"

"I don't want her arrested? I just want my car back?"

"But you say she's been threatening you."

"Everyone threatens me? Bo says that's how we know I'm doing something right?"

Bo smiled at him like a proud papa.

"Just get my car back?" the kid said. "Without the police, okay?"

*

The walls were pink and covered with scholastic awards, honors certificates, cutout pictures of musicians. Surprising ones: Big Mama Thornton, Bo Diddley, the Beatles, both Elvises.

But no sign of Brandon G, which could explain the threats, the break-in, the car theft. Hell hath no fury like a former fan.

@All4Leyna's real name was Leyna Escovedo, and she lived in Seaford, one town over from Brandon. It had taken Rico fifteen minutes on his laptop to trace her location from pictures she'd posted on social media.

Probably because we looked and sounded like cops, her mother let us in without question and brought us upstairs to see the young woman's room.

"I don't know where she is," Mrs. Escovedo said. "If you can find her, that would be nice. Just to let me know she's okay. I worry."

She didn't seem very worried.

"Does your daughter have a driver's license?" I said.

"Of course. She's eighteen, not an idiot."

"This is not the first time she's taken off?"

"At least twice a summer since she *got* her license."

"She have a car?"

"Did you happen to notice we don't have a mailbox out by the curb? You can see the hole where it was. I'm waiting on my husband to call someone to replace it. You want to guess what happened to it during graduation week last month? No, my daughter no longer has a car."

I thanked Mrs. Escovedo for her time, took her information. Back in our car, I asked Rico if he wanted to do some legwork.

*

When I think about the sunset of my career—and I try *not* to think of it often—I never think how much fun it will be to obsessively go through a teenager's social-media posts.

Leyna's were full of pictures and videos of musicians, old timers like Sister Rosetta Tharpe, Little Richard, Johnny Cash, Carl Perkins, Chuck Berry.

But that had changed two months earlier, when post after post of Brandon G began popping up. Like she had caught a bug and gone feverish. Then, two weeks ago, the posts changed: she started making fun of his haircut, his music. And *then* things turned vicious:

your career iz over

someone needz to take you off the scene

Finally, last night, she'd gone over the edge.

She'd posted a picture of Brandon's Continental. Underneath it, she'd written:

gonna sett this on fire. 2 bad Brandon wont be in it when I due

*

Rico called from Asbury Park, where he was checking hotels. "This is where she came last summer," he said. "No sign of her, though."

"You check out the Stone Pony? Something tells me our Leyna might like it there. I went to so many shows back in the day. You ever see Springsteen live? It's like a—"

"Bobby, no offense, but I just spent four hours in traffic. I gotta get home tonight or the wife'll kill me."

"Okay," I said. "Keep at it."

*

At the Gamberini residence, we rotated four-man teams around the clock, placed surveillance cameras around the property, and shadowed Brandon wherever he went—which mainly meant the Sunrise Mall every afternoon.

The kid had scored a booking on *Good Morning America*, though. I spent a few days smoothing out details with security at ABC's Times Square studio, and on the day of, things were going fine. The kid was in the private dressing room he had demanded. Diane was in the green room, and I found Mitch standing at the edge of the set as it was being prepped. Gleaming glass, massive equipment, an army of people in headsets moving back and forth.

"This is amazing," he said.

"It's pretty far from the dive bars in Suffolk County."

"Very far. You know, I was just a schmuck at school, a schmegdorf who lucked into a hot band. But I was going down a bad path. I was snorting, smoking, shooting. Diane saved me from myself. Every groupie and her sister had their claws out for me. She's been my soul mate, through and through."

I nodded. I had known some of that, but I hadn't been enough of a friend to help. I didn't know what to say, and my instincts were telling me I should do another sweep of the place, so I went with something trite. "It's nice to see how well things have worked out for you two."

"To be honest," he said with a heavy sigh, "I think she's going to leave me. That on top of pressure pills and medical bills, I wish I could enjoy this moment more."

Now I *really* had nothing useful to say. But I was curious. "I thought the kid was doing okay, moneywise."

"*He* is. But the way his manager has things set up, the money isn't trickling down. And I laid out a lot to get him started. He's a good kid, but selfish. We both know how it is at that age."

"Age doesn't ma—"

We were interrupted by a scream.

A production manager was kneeling in front of our boy's dressing room. On the ground, facedown, wedged in by the door, was Doug from the agency. His leg was bleeding bad.

"Stabbed," he groaned. "From behind."

"The kid?" I said.

"Inside. Sorry, Bobby."

I pushed the door open and found the room empty. "What the hell?"

Just then an inner door opened and the kid stepped out in a robe, his hair wrapped in a towel. He was trailed by steam that smelled like hibiscus. "Whoa? I'm not dressed?"

"Oh, my god!" Diane yelled, pushing past me. "My baby! Are you okay?" She turned to yell at me. "Where were you people? What are we paying you for?"

Mitch rushed in after her.

"Brandon's fine," I said.

"No thanks to you," he said.

They were raw with fear, hugging their son and ignoring the man on the floor who might have saved the kid's life just by being there.

Doug's partner David called me over to the dressing-room table. "Check this out."

The note was straight out of a movie, with letters cut from magazines. It read: *Deth 2 BRANDON!*

*

After a four-hour debriefing with the police—three of which were spent kibbitzing—I checked on Doug at Mount Sinai West. His wound was serious, and he would be out of commission for at least a week. He said he was more embarrassed than anything else, didn't know how some teenage girl had surprised him. I told him I was wondering about that, too.

From the hospital, I drove back to the Gamberinis'.

There was still a cohort of reporters in front. One of our guys let me inside. He had a better-watch-out look in his eyes, and when I entered the living room I realized what he was warning me about. Diane was sitting thigh-to-thigh with Bo, her arm behind him and their faces very close.

I flashed back to a time I had caught her and Mitch doing the same thing on the couch of our suite at Stony Brook. How they found time to study—him a music major, her in Computer Science—I'll never know.

"Sorry to interrupt," I said.

"Bobby! Oh, my god!" she said, getting up and taking my hands in hers. "I'm glad you're here. I'm sorry I got on your case this morning. I get very emotional."

"No worries. It's completely understandable."

"But you need to catch this Leyna. She's obviously dangerous."

"We have an operative on her trail, Diane, and the police are after her, too. It's just a matter of time."

"Did you know she and my Brandon were an item?"

"They dated? I did not know that."

"You see her motive now, right? You understand why she wants to harm my son?"

"Is Mitch around?" I asked, pretty sure I knew the answer.

Bo, the producer-manager, got up and came over to me.

"Ah, Mr. Lavoe," he said, putting a hand on my shoulder and leaning close. Bourbon today. "If I could have a word."

He led me into a hallway off the kitchen and peeked back into the living room to make sure the coast was clear. "I know what that looked like back there. I don't want you to think something is going on."

"It's not my job to judge, Bo."

"Yes, well, I assure you I'm not sure myself what's going on. Let me put it this way. Brandon is a very sensitive young man. And where is his father? Probably out hunting for that stupid car. He's obsessed with it. It seems I'm one of the few people who genuinely care about Brandon's well-being and success."

"A lot of manager-producers say they feel that way."

"Haw haw," he said, removing his hand from my shoulder. "I see you've made up your mind. In any case, I understand how hard your job is, and I want to say that I at least appreciate what you're doing."

"Sure thing," I said, eager to get away from him. "I'm going to go check on Brandon now."

*

Brandon lived in his parents' finished basement. A drum kit, a series of guitars, and an electric keyboard took up one side of the space. On the other side was an unmade king-sized bed and, facing it, a TV screen about the size of a football field.

Lying on the floor with his feet on the bed, Brandon G strummed a guitar and sang.

It's hard to describe the sound. It was as if Jiminy Cricket had just awakened after a long night of drinking and smoking.

But, honestly, I've heard worse.

When he stopped, I asked him where his father was.

He didn't get up. "Uh, no idea?" he said.

He seemed about to go back to strumming, so I said, "I heard you and this Leyna used to date."

"I guess?"

"How did you meet, if I may ask?"

"She was interviewing me for a report or an essay or something? It was homework? She's so weird, like, she's a straight-A student?"

"Can you tell me why you broke up with her?"

"She's the one who broke up with me?"

"That's news. Why would she do that?"

"I don't know," he said, not in form of a question. "I miss her. I miss her all the time."

My phone beeped. Rico.

"Bobby. Days Inn, Copiague. Manager says she's been here for a week, signed in as Sparkle Moore."

"Sparkle Moore? Is she there now?"

"No, but she hasn't checked out, and her stuff is still in the room."

"All right. Send me the address."

I disconnected the call.

"Did you find her?" Brandon said. "Can I come with you?"

"Good questions," I said. "Maybe, and no."

*

I parked just down the street from the motel, and Rico jumped into my car.

"Cannata's in the parking lot, and Liberty has been standing in the lobby looking at brochures for an hour."

At that moment, we got a signal from Cannata that the girl registered as Sparkle Moore was exiting the premises via a back door.

"She spotted me," he said. "She's running. I'm right behind her."

A second later, a car raced past us, screeching rubber.

It was a cherry-red sports coupe.

"That's no baby-blue Continental," I said into my phone.

"It's her BFF's," Cannata told me, squealing by me. "Shoshona Martling. They've been staying here together."

"We have to stop using black SUVs for surveillance," I said. "They're a dead giveaway."

I did a U-turn and gunned it.

"You think she trashed the Continental?" Rico said.

"Whoa!" I spun the wheel to get past a truck that was backing up. "Maybe. I have my doubts."

Another sharp turn. We merged onto Sunrise Highway—where Leyna stepped on the gas.

"She's doing ninety," I said, cutting in front of a delivery-truck driver, who gave me a long honk.

"What doubts, Bobby?"

"The social-media posts, the misspellings, the note. It's too predictable. Too sloppy."

"Kids today—"

"Don't underestimate them. And you saw her room. The awards. The fact she knows about Sparkle Moore."

Leyna took Route 110 toward the Southern State. She bobbed and weaved, but that cherry red was easy to track.

Sirens. The cops. It was only a matter of time before a helicopter got in on the act.

The chase didn't last long. Just before we hit the Wantagh State Parkway, she seemed to lose heart. She slowed down and pulled over.

Smart, I thought. This could've ended with her crushed into a median.

I stopped the car and waited. The cops were in charge now.

*

Two hours and a lot of chitchat later, Rico and I were led into an interview room. Leyna Escovedo sat there, arms crossed. She had curly brown hair and eyes that laser-focused on us. When the officer in charge explained who we were, she looked like she wanted to rip our spines in half. I think Rico actually took a step back.

"You don't get it! I'm so over Brandon! My account was hacked, weeks ago! Someone keeps posting all this crap about him, and then I started getting death threats from all Brandon's stans! I was afraid for my life!"

"So you don't have the Continental?"

"I can't drive a stick," she said. "If you ask me, his idiot producer's behind this stuff."

"Bo? Why?"

She looked at me like I was the idiot. "To drum up publicity, duh. It's Marketing 101."

"That's not a bad theory. Listen, I'm sorry for all the hassle, but you could've saved yourself a lot of trouble."

She hung her head and dropped the attitude. "Honestly, it was fun hiding out. And I got to do a car chase! None of my friends can say that! Look, with Brandon, we had a thing, yes. I liked him. I *really* liked him. But when I got hacked, he wouldn't believe me. I'm sure that was his mom's fault. She hates me. I brought her a tray of my mother's homemade lasagna, and she refused to eat it. Anyway, I would never get so wrapped up in a guy I would break into his house."

I didn't want to smile, but I did. "Nice touch with Sparkle Moore."

"Thank you," she said. "Not enough people know who she is."

Back in the car, I told Rico I had a little more digging for him to do.

*

Porky's was still on Central Avenue. In 1980, it had been the best joint in town, crowded with drinkers as underage as I was and local bands desperate to hit it big. Bands like the Eternal Neanderthals.

When I swung open the door, I was sad to see it had become a typical Long Island bar: big-screen TVs, sports logos everywhere you looked, a selection of local taps. The place must still pack them in at night, but at two in the afternoon in the middle of the week there were only a few day-drunks spaced along the bar and a bartender with a hook for a left hand.

The couple I was there to see was by the rear window, parked in front of what looked liked crème de menthes.

I pulled up a third chair and saw the baby-blue Continental parked out back.

I called for a beer and another round for the soulmates.

"Thank you for meeting me," I said. "Who wants to speak first?"

Mitch shrugged. "We never meant it to go this far. Things got out of hand. Who knew it would blow up so much?"

"I started it," Diane said quietly. She wasn't being flirty or touchy now. "When I met that Leyna, I knew she was trouble because she reminded me of, well, *me*. And I didn't think Brandon was ready. He's still a child."

"So you hacked her phone."

"It was easy. I sent her a text from Brandon's phone, with a link. When she clicked on it, I was in."

"I was reminded this morning that you were a Computer Science major at Stony Brook. You made a career of it for a while."

"It's the one thing I've always been really good at."

"Good enough to change grades so you and your soulmate could graduate college?"

"Oh, my god! How did you—?"

"A guess. So you just wanted Leyna out of the way? What was the deal with the car?"

"That's where I came in," Mitch said. "I found out what Diane had done and, well, we were only having fun. I didn't think we were hurting anyone. Brandon and Leyna would get over it. Listen, we spoiled him rotten, gave the kid whatever he wanted. I just wanted to drive the car sometimes, but he wouldn't let me. My own son!"

Diane put her hand on mine. "Mitch's father treated him badly, never let him drive that stupid car while he was alive, and then it was Brandon's and *again* he wasn't allowed to drive it. That's all there was to it."

"Not quite," I said. "You threatened your own son. And you stabbed one of my guys so you could plant that fake note."

Diane hung her head. "I didn't mean to. But he was standing there *texting* when he was supposed to be guarding Brandon!"

"And you happened to have a knife on you?"

"I grew up in Riverhead. I've carried a knife since I was twelve."

"You were both surprised when I showed up that first day. You didn't know what I'd do if I found out. Then you tried to throw me off the scent, first Mitch weeping about your leaving him and then you fake-canoodling with the Brit."

"Who says I was faking?" she said.

"Diane!" Mitch said.

"Sorry," she said, winking at him.

They were like two children, and I was tired of their games. "Listen up. Doug's okay, and I'm sure he'd rather not press charges.

Neither would the company. As far as the Continental goes, you can say someone else took it for a joyride and then returned it. But the ethical thing to do would be tell the cops."

"Oh, my god!"

"Either way," I said, taking a slug of my beer, which was flat, "you're going tell *Brandon* what you did—"

"We can't! He'll hate us."

I got up from the table, thought about throwing down some money for our drinks, decided against it.

"—and then you're going to invite Leyna over to the house. And if she brings her mama's lasagna again, you're going to eat the whole damn thing."

The Nylon Curtain
Released September 1982

"Allentown"
"Laura"
"Pressure"
"Goodnight Saigon"
"She's Right on Time"
"A Room of Our Own"
"Surprises"
"Scandinavian Skies"
"Where's the Orchestra?"

All songs by Billy Joel.

Goodnight Saigon
by Richard Helms

The first person Owen Wheeler met upon walking off the plane into a solid wall of heat and humidity at Bien Hoa Airport was Bud Abraham, a tall, slender black man who escorted him to the divisional barracks. A seasoned veteran, Bud had survived five Long Range Recon Patrols—*lurps,* for short. A lurp might take four days, sometimes five, during which the patrol's only link to the relative safety of its base was its radioman. American soldiers weren't yet combatants in Vietnam. Their primary role was to help prepare and advise Vietnamese soldiers to defend their own country from the PLAF insurgents, but once the black flag rose and the bullets flew, every man in a uniform was fair game. Bud had already seen several patrol buddies go home in plastic bags with numbers stenciled on them.

Wheeler had spent his entire first tour in Germany as part of the eternal occupational force there, soaking up beer and enjoying the company of a seemingly endless procession of Teutonic beauties. Reenlisting had been a mistake. He scoured his memory for any unintentional insult he might have delivered to justify his being relegated to a trivia-question country at the ass end of Indochina.

Never having faced an enemy in combat, Wheeler was petrified. He wasn't the only one. A guy named Charlie five bunks down whispered prayers for an hour each night before falling into fitful sleep—impassioned pleas to allow him to survive just one more lurp. Wheeler caught another kid, Baker, crying in the shower, scouring his skin, trying to remove imaginary blood. It would be years before Bob Hope would venture into the country with an entourage of *Playboy* bunnies to cheer up the troops. In 1958, all the terrified soldiers had for solace was each other.

A month later, after four lurps of his own, Wheeler was still alive and becoming familiar with the routine. It didn't make things easier.

Bud Abraham poked his head around the corner.

"Got a briefing," he said. He didn't need to say more.

They were headed back to the jungle.

*

A De Havilland Beaver dropped them in a clearing outside a no-name *ville* deep in the jungle. Their commander was a first lieutenant named Riley, only a few months older than them. Riley had recently graduated from the University of Michigan with a degree in economics, which—in the Army's obtuse calculus—perfectly suited him for combat command.

Five green ARVN recruits, most of them conscripted from the Vietnamese highlands, waited to be marched in a large circle through the jungle, eventually arriving back at the *ville*. Along the way, the Americans would demonstrate warcraft and survival skills, so, when the real thing came along, the recruits would be marginally less likely to be slaughtered.

First, Wheeler had to teach the ARVN boys to pack their gear. Packing was always a trade-off. If you couldn't find vital equipment in a poorly packed ruck when things went south, you died. They carried food and ammunition. Pack too little of either, and you died. There were dozens of ways to die on a lurp, and it was Wheeler's and Bud's job to teach the ARVN pukes how to avoid them.

Riley took the lead, with Bud in the rear, carrying the radio. Wheeler and the ARVN conscripts spread out in the middle. It was a miserable business. The entire countryside conspired to impede them. Vines grew across every path, ready to snare a man's foot and send him sprawling. Holes covered with fallen leaves waited patiently to break an ankle. Tripping over rocks was commonplace. The typical four-day lurp was a constant battle against terrain, mosquitoes, wild animals, fungus, poisonous plants, and—if you were truly unfortunate—stray Viet Cong patrols. At night, they ate cold food from tins and drank sparingly.

"Tents are for pussies," Bud informed the recruits. "On a patrol, you make yourself comfortable as you can against a tree or a rock, keep your weapon and ruck immediately available, and grab whatever shut-eye you can between watches and nightmares."

They lost a man the first night. Around one in the morning, one of the conscripts slipped out of the tiny clearing to relieve himself. He didn't hear the *chuff* off to his right or see the yellow eyes following his movements through the trees. He didn't hear the padded footfalls tracking him.

His screams woke the camp, followed by a horrifying roar and a thrashing in the jungle. One of the ARVN soldiers grabbed his carbine and set off to help his comrade. Bud seized him by the ankle and dragged him back.

"Don't bother," he said. "Dude's dead already. You can't fault the tiger. He only wants to eat, same as us."

After sunup, they divided the dead man's rations, buried the rest of his ruck, and humped another twelve miles.

They made camp near sundown in a small clearing on the edge of the jungle. Exhausted, they wolfed some rations and collapsed against trees to rest before beginning the circular trek back to the *ville* at daybreak.

Two hours later, they were rattled awake by the sound of the ARVN lookout firing on full automatic. Bud leapt to his feet and grabbed the carbine from him. The soldier trembled, pointing into the undergrowth, and shouted, *"Con hổ!"*

"Tiger," Riley interpreted.

"Stupid fuck!" Bud shouted. "Why don't you just radio the VC and give them our position?"

The man started to answer, but a bullet screamed in from the brush and spattered his brains over the campsite, accented by the delayed sonic whipcrack of a rifle.

"Incoming!" Riley cried. They hit the dirt and grabbed for their weapons. Two more muted slaps broke the silence. Bullets whistled over their heads.

"Radio base," Riley ordered. "Give them our position and tell them we're under fire. We need a gunship and exfil here, pronto!" He turned to Wheeler. "How many you think are out there?"

"Beats me, Loot. Might be a single sniper. Could be a whole fuckin' platoon."

"We're sitting ducks in this clearing. Let's get into the brush."

They fanned out in a loose semicircle.

"Any luck?" Riley rasped.

"They're on the way," Bud said. "Twenty minutes out."

"Let's see what we're up against. Everyone fire a short burst in that direction."

Their rifles spat out a quick volley, and Riley held up his hand. Five distinct flashes blazed from different locations, maybe seventy yards away.

Riley gestured to the ARVN conscripts to rotate to the right, deeper into the jungle. In the faint moonlight, Wheeler could see their terrified faces. One of them dropped his rifle, held up his hands, and shouted in Vietnamese. He ran into the jungle in the direction of the firing and was cut down.

"Guess negotiation is out of the question," Bud said calmly. He drew a bead, squeezed off a two-shot burst in the direction of the flash, and was rewarded by a truncated scream in the distance.

"Four more," Riley said. "Unless they have a sniper posted nearby."

"If they did, we'd be dead already," Bud said. "Support's fifteen minutes out."

"Keep moving," Riley ordered. "Stay near the clearing. It's the only place the Beaver can land. Bud, tell the jet pilot to light up everything ain't within thirty yards of the clearing."

One of the VC soldiers swept the area with a Type 56. Bud, bringing up the rear with the radio set, was hit on the right side. The bullet exited his back and lodged in his ruck. He collapsed onto his stomach.

"Hit!" he yelled.

Wheeler crawled back on his belly. Riley and the ARVN Rangers returned fire. Wheeler dug through Bud's ruck for something to stanch the bleeding.

A Viet Cong soldier sprang from the underbrush ten yards from Bud and Wheeler, his rifle raised to fire. On adrenalin-pumped reflex, Wheeler swung his M14 around and shot the man high in the chest, just under the collarbone. He crumpled to the ground, screaming in pain. Riley jumped onto him and ripped the rifle from his hands.

"Jesus," Riley muttered. "He's a kid, can't be older than fourteen."

The drone of the Beaver's Y6G rotary engine rose in the distance, along with the high-pitched roar of F-86 Sabres.

"Get to the clearing!" Riley shouted. "There might be more of them in the jungle. We don't want to be in the weeds when the jet arrives." He pointed toward the VC insurgent Wheeler had shot. "I'll help Bud. You drag this asshole, Wheeler. Intelligence might be able to get something useful out of him."

*

"You'll be back in Georgia in a couple of weeks," Wheeler told Bud, back at the base hospital. "You saved us all, getting the Beaver to pick us up. Shame you passed out. You should have seen it, man. The fast movers swooped in over the trees, fifty-calibers blazing, phosphorous tracers lighting up the sky. The jungle looked like a cornfield back home when the harvester hits it. Never saw the like of it in my life. If any VC were coming to help their buddies, they're little greasy puddles now."

A nurse stopped by Bud's bed and checked his vital signs. She was cute.

But Wheeler was exhausted and looked eight kinds of ugly. He needed a shower. He could smell his own stink. It wouldn't be a great time to hit on her.

The nurse smiled at him and turned to leave, but another nurse stopped her.

"We're almost out of B-positive blood," the older nurse said. "Why don't you ask around, see if anyone can donate?"

Seeing the opportunity to score some points, Wheeler stood up. "I'm B-positive."

"Thanks, but I don't think so," the cute nurse told him. "After three days of rations and bad water, you're probably dehydrated."

"Could use a bath and a meal I don't have to break into with a can opener, but I feel strong, and I'm ready to help."

The two nurses looked at one another, and the older one said, "Any other time, I'd turn you down, but a patient in surgery needs B-positive badly. Come on."

Wheeler smiled at the cute nurse. She smiled back. Maybe he had a shot, after all.

"Who's in surgery?" he asked, passing the time, as she prepared the needle to draw his blood.

"That Vietnamese kid you brought in from the jungle. You'll feel a little pinch...."

*

Riley stuck his head around the corner later that evening. He looked worried. "Wheeler. Got a minute?"

Wheeler followed the lieutenant to a hut where Riley shared a hot desk with four other officers. An ARVN colonel—Wheeler could tell by the three blossoms on the officer's olive-drab blouse collar—stood and greeted them.

"This is the man?" the colonel asked.

"Specialist Wheeler," Riley told him. "He helped me bring the boy back."

"I am Colonel Thanh," he said, shaking Wheeler's hand. The colonel's English was faultless. "I would like to thank you, not only for helping Lieutenant Riley retrieve a valuable asset, but also for keeping him alive for interrogation. I am informed you gave your own blood to save his life. Admirable. We extracted a great deal of information from the traitorous scum, information which may prove beneficial in breaking the back of the PLAF insurgency."

"I'm pleased I was able to help. I regret we lost three of your men in the jungle."

"Casualties are an unfortunate fact of life in war, Specialist Wheeler. Now, if you will excuse me, I have unpleasant business to which I must attend." He turned to Riley. "We have obtained everything necessary from your prisoner. I have two sergeants retrieving him now. I accept transfer to our custody. Thank you again, Lieutenant."

"Anytime," Riley said.

*

"What's going on?" Wheeler asked, when Colonel Thanh was gone.

"You heard him. He's taking the prisoner."

"Where?"

"He isn't taking him anywhere, Wheeler. He's just *taking* him."

Riley gazed out the window. Wheeler watched over his shoulder. Two ARVN sergeants dragged the wounded kid across the compound, his bare toes dragging in the dirt. The gauze bandage over his surgery incision was splotched with fresh wet blood. The boy's skin was pale in the razor-sharp sunlight. His hair hung like sodden twine on his forehead. His eyes drooped from the pain-killing drugs in his system. Wheeler wondered whether he knew what was happening.

"We can't let them do this, sir," Wheeler said. "This is wrong."

"We're visitors, here by invitation." Riley's voice was mournful. "We can't interfere. We don't make the rules here, and we sure as shit don't impose our rules on them. The Geneva Conventions don't cover treason. Justice for traitors in this country is firm and quick. The boy was tried and convicted the instant he put on those black pajamas."

The ARVN sergeants caught up with Colonel Thanh. They propped the kid against a tree. Thanh walked up to the kid, drew his pistol, and—without a second's hesitation—parked a bullet between his eyes. The boy's body slumped to the ground, and Thanh squeezed two more rounds into the back of his head.

Wheeler watched through tears as blood—so recently his *own* blood—pooled in the dust at the base of the tree. Thanh barked an order to the sergeants and walked away. The sergeants each grabbed an ankle and dragged the body off to be disposed.

"This isn't our war," Riley said. There was a catch in his voice.

"Kind of feels like it is, sir."

"You've been through a lot," Riley said. "I'm authorizing a five-day pass. Go into Saigon. Drink a case of beer. Get your ashes hauled. Say goodbye to Bud before you go. He'll be halfway Stateside when you get back."

*

Among the first actions Ngo Dinh Diem took as prime minister of South Vietnam in 1954 was to close the Binh Xuyen casinos. This proved an unpopular measure, and by 1958 the gambling houses had begun to reopen with a somewhat lower profile than before. Wheeler found himself in one of them, accessed through the back of a *pho* house.

He wandered over to a *pai gow* table manned by a bald one-eyed dealer. Wheeler could have spent most of the evening there for the equivalent of US taxi fare. He played listlessly, never betting more than the table minimum, fully aware that the Binh Xuyen mob was under no obligation to keep the game fair. He was killing time, and gambling was a hell of a lot cheaper and healthier than hiring one of the blown-out, pox-ridden prostitutes who loitered in his hotel lobby.

He had been at the table for almost an hour when a man in uniform slid onto the chair beside him. Wheeler glanced at him and did a double take.

"Colonel Thanh!" he said. Thanh was the last person Wheeler would have expected to find in a semi-legitimate Saigon casino, especially wearing ARVN fatigues and the three-flower insignia.

The man appeared half-snockered. He turned toward Wheeler and squinted.

"Yes?" he said. "You look familiar. Wait. It's Wheeler, right? Specialist Wheeler?"

"Yes, sir."

"I saw you a couple of days ago, at the American emplacement in—"

"That's right, sir."

"Yes," Thanh said, drawing the word out. "I recall now. Nasty business, that. Where are you from, Wheeler?"

"North Carolina. A small town called Prosperity. I'm sure you've never heard of it."

"Don't be so certain. I spent a great deal of time in the States. Went to college there."

"Where?"

"Hofstra University. Long Island, New York. Go, Flying Dutchmen. I lived off campus with three other guys. Had an apartment about six miles from the university. Place called Hicksville. I'm sure you've never heard of it."

"Explains why your English is so good," Wheeler said.

He realized he and Thanh must be almost the same age. He'd been fooled by the rank, but as a slightly inebriated Thanh reminisced about his college days on Long Island, his features softened, shed the mask of war, and revealed a youthful face. Wheeler could imagine Thanh dressed in a Hawaiian shirt and chinos and Bass Weejuns, yukking it up at a kegger with a bunch of Hofstra frat boys, not a care in the world. A guy like that, Wheeler wouldn't mind hanging out with.

Didn't really matter, though. Wheeler had already decided to kill the man.

*

As Thanh prattled on, Wheeler worked out a plan.

He wasn't completely certain why the colonel had to die, beyond the fact that killing the VC kid had rendered Wheeler's sanguine sacrifice a waste. Perhaps it was the way Thanh had summarily shot him, without a single sign of pity or remorse. Wheeler wondered how many children Thanh had executed since the beginning of the conflict.

Owen Wheeler had grown to hate everything about this godforsaken jungle hellhole, and perhaps Thanh was just the unlucky bastard who was going to carry the weight for it.

Whatever the reason, Thanh was going to die. The question was *how*. Infantrymen weren't typically issued side arms, and, even if he had one, Wheeler wouldn't be carrying it on leave. Besides, guns were messy and loud. Shooting Thanh would draw too much attention in the packed Saigon streets.

Thanh gazed at him curiously. "Is something wrong?" he asked. "You look ... troubled. Are you thinking about the kid the other day?"

"What about him?" Wheeler asked.

Several feet away, the bartender sliced limes and lemons with a six-inch knife. Wheeler watched him and remembered the admonition of one of the drill sergeants teaching hand-to-hand at Parris Island: *There is no body cavity or major organ that cannot be reached by a five-inch blade and a good stout arm.*

The bartender's knife would give him an inch to spare.

Thanh's glass was almost empty.

"Let me get the next round," Wheeler said.

"Thanks. I'll be right back. Have to milk the dragon." Thanh slapped Wheeler's arm with inebriated collegiality and headed for the men's room.

Wheeler ordered a couple of drafts. Watching the bartender draw them, he laid a hand over the untended knife, slid it across the bar, and secreted it in the front pocket of his chinos. He pulled out his shirttail to cover the wooden hilt.

This would work, he reasoned. They'd drink a little more, and then Wheeler would suggest they take a trip down the street to a brothel for some friendly and cheap companionship. When they were in the empty alley, Wheeler would throw an arm around Thanh's shoulder, a comradely gesture, and plunge the blade into Thanh's stomach. He fantasized Thanh's eyes growing wide with pain and terror, the confused look that would cross his face.

Yeah, he would say. *I'm thinking about the kid the other day.*

*

After they drained their beers, Wheeler made his play. Thanh bought in immediately, delighted to share an adventure with his new American buddy. Wheeler's heart pounded, and an adrenalin roar in his ears—like ocean waves—drowned out the din of the casino.

As they approached the door to the alley, their progress was impeded by two ARVN MPs. A freezing cascade of panic rose in Wheeler's chest. Was it possible they knew what he was up to? No, that was irrational. The Vietnamese weren't psychic.

The taller MP stood in front of them. The smaller one hung back to keep an eye on the room. The tall one barked something in Vietnamese, and Wheeler recognized the tone of an order. Thanh became drunkenly indignant, but the MP was unimpressed and insistent. He took Thanh by the arm, squeezing so tightly that Thanh winced.

Thanh turned to Wheeler. "These men are arresting me," he explained. "They say I have conspired with the Viet Cong. Tell them you know me. Tell them you saw me execute that traitorous VC scum only a few days ago."

Wheeler relived the mental image of the boy lying at Thanh's feet, their mixed blood soaking into the dirt, and he smiled.

"Sounds like a personal problem to me," he said. "Hope you work it out."

He pushed past the MPs into the alley and dumped the knife in the first trash heap he passed.

*

When he returned to the encampment, Wheeler found Lieutenant Riley at his desk, reading a dispatch.

"Thanh's been arrested," the lieutenant said.

"I was there. Ran into him in a casino in Saigon. We had a drink or two. They arrested him shortly after."

"I see. You know I speak Vietnamese?"

"Yes."

"Thanh didn't. He made a mistake, letting me watch the interrogation of that kid you saved. He didn't kill the kid because of the insurgency. The kid recognized him. Knew about him. He expected Thanh to protect him. Instead, Thanh killed him to shut him up."

"You could have stopped it," Wheeler protested.

"I could have. But then what? He's a colonel in another army. I had no hold on him. After I sent you to Saigon, I contacted his superiors. They took over from there. How did he look when they arrested him?"

"Scared shitless," Wheeler said, "and guilty as hell."

Riley nodded, and Wheeler thought he saw the hint of a smile form at the corners of his mouth. "Good," he said. "I called you in here for this."

Riley reached into his desk drawer and handed Wheeler a small box. It contained a red ribbon with gold braid.

"I put you in for the Meritorious Unit Commendation for what you did out on the lurp, saving Bud and bringing in the kid. Donating your own blood to save his life uncovered a traitor in the ARVN. Take it. You earned it."

Recalling how he had planned to murder Thanh, Wheeler was ashamed. "I—I don't deserve this, Loot. When I was in Saigon with Thanh, I—I planned—"

"I don't give a damn what you planned in Saigon," Riley told him. "And neither does anyone else. Take the commendation, Specialist. That's an order."

"Yes, sir," Wheeler said, and pocketed the box.

"One other thing. Whatever fuckery got your ass sent here has been wiped clean. You have new orders." He handed Wheeler the dispatch he'd been reading. "Tokyo. You leave on the next transport out, at fourteen hundred hours. Better start packing. All I can say is, you're one lucky bastard. First night in the Ginza, toss one back for me, okay?"

*

Wheeler walked toward the yawning front-loading bay of the C-124 Globemaster at Bien Hoa Airport, all his equipment packed into a single heavy duffel. He took a seat on a row of webbing racks in the spartan interior. A kid who looked seventeen checked to see that he and the five other soldiers were secure. The plane rose into the sky and flew southward.

"Headed to Tokyo, huh?" the kid said.

"Yeah," Wheeler said.

"Were you deployed in country? Is it bad as they say?"

"Diogenes searched every street and alley of Athens for a completely honest man. Never found one. He set the bar too high, kid. The jungle makes heroes and monsters. Sometimes it's hard to figure out which one you are."

The kid stared at him for a moment, confused. He shook his head and walked away to take his own seat.

Several minutes later, they passed over the city. Wheeler peered out one of the ports, looking down on the lights.

"Goodnight, Saigon," he said.

An Innocent Man
Released August 1983

"Easy Money"
"An Innocent Man"
"The Longest Time"
"This Night"
"Tell Her About It"
"Uptown Girl"
"Careless Talk"
"Christie Lee"
"Leave a Tender Moment Alone"
"Keeping the Faith"

All songs by Billy Joel
(except for the chorus to "This Night,"
which is credited to L. v. Beethoven).

Easy Money
by John M. Floyd

Rick Harrelson, barely awake, stared through the passenger-side window of Bobby Joe Faraday's truck at a landscape he'd known all his life. Thickets of oak and sweet gum, streamers of Spanish moss, hills dotted with redbud and dogwood, valleys choked with kudzu, all of it flowing past at a bumpy fifty miles an hour. In different weather and at a different time of day, it might've been a pleasant view. At six o'clock on an overcast morning with ninety-percent humidity, it was just a stretch of damp gray backwoods. He was already sweating, and he hadn't even put the suit on yet.

The suit.

How in God's name had he let himself get talked into this?

"Is it too late to back out?" he asked.

Bobby Joe gave him a look. "I hope you're joking. You told Lorena you'd do it, and she's paying you for it."

"Yep, that's me: I'm a man who can't say no," Rick said. "But you're the one I told, and you said *you'll* be paying me."

"With her money."

Rick sighed. In his opinion, his old pal Bobby Joe Faraday, Jr., had sold his soul when he went to work for Gatewood Chemical. Lorena Smith Gatewood and her empire owned almost everything as far as you could see in Harris County, Mississippi, though the towering pines and looming tangles of kudzu usually kept that to a short distance. She certainly owned Bobby Joe, and probably this snazzy black truck of his, too. Rick's own vehicle was a twenty-three-year-old Toyota with a weak battery, which was the reason he was riding with his friend.

If you could call him a friend, after this.

Rick found himself wondering if *he* was the one who'd sold his soul, and for only a thousand dollars at that. At the time, it had sounded like easy money.

"Tell me again," he said, "why Her Highness wants this done."

"I told you all I know. The owner of this stretch of land wants to put a casino here, and Lorena doesn't want him to. What you're gonna do today should stop it."

Rick frowned. "I thought Lorena—G-Chem—owned all the land around here."

"Not this piece."

"But why wouldn't she want a casino built? She doesn't strike me as a conservationist. Or a moralist, either."

"Beats me," Bobby Joe said. "Ask your sister. She works for Lorena, too."

Rick shook his head. "Jenny and I haven't kept in touch. Besides, she's an accountant. She wouldn't know about this kind of thing."

"You think *I* do? I'm just a foot soldier, Rick, carrying out orders."

Rick didn't reply to that. Instead he said, "Looks like you lost one of your fancy buttons."

Bobby Joe glanced down, surprised, at the open cuff of his right sleeve. The buttons on his Western-cut shirt *were* fancy—like little shiny pearls. He rolled up the buttonless sleeve and pointed past the windshield. "We're here," he said.

They parked and climbed out onto a soggy clearing on the east bank of Drowning Creek, one of those middle-of-nowhere streams that someone had long ago deemed not quite impressive enough to be called a river. But it was thirty feet wide at this point, and flowing fast and loud. Rick thought it looked eager to live up to its name. Birds screamed with irritating enthusiasm in the treetops, and everything smelled damp and earthy, a combination of scents Rick usually liked.

The back seat of the extended-cab pickup held, among other things, a Saints ball cap, an expensive camera, a fishing rod, a scoped 30.06 rifle, and an Army blanket. Hidden beneath the blanket was Rick's gear: a roll of twine, two snowshoe-like paddles with holes punched in the sides, a pair of homemade shoes, woolly gloves, and a hooded ankle-length coat of brown hair.

Without a word, he unloaded the twine, shoes, paddles, gloves, and coat, and spread them out on the hood of the truck.

The costume Bobby Joe had found for him—probably meant for someone playing a bear or gorilla on stage—would be hot, but at least it buttoned down the front like a jacket, so he wouldn't have to climb into it like coveralls.

He held out his hand and said, "Knife."

With Bobby Joe's pocketknife, Rick cut lengths of twine and threaded them through the holes in the burlap "shoes" he'd made for the occasion. To these he attached the wooden cutouts, each in the shape of a ten-inch-wide, thirty-inch-long humanlike foot. Then he sat in the grass and strapped the heavy paddles to his feet like sandals. He tried not to think much about the craziness of what he was doing.

What Bobby Joe hadn't said was that Lorena Gatewood didn't want her neighbor Walter Burchfield building a casino because she wanted to build one herself, on her own land, ten miles north. Drowning Creek might not be a river, but it was big enough to justify a casino, which by Mississippi law must be located on a body of water. And since there'd been reported sightings of a southern version of Bigfoot in the area, Lorena had decided to fan those flames. Weird redneck publicity would make Walter's already cautious investors look for a less controversial site—like the one Lorena owned upstream.

Today's plan was for Rick to head north in full costume along the creek bank, leaving monster-sized footprints, while Bobby Joe took long-range photos from the woods on the far side of the creek. Afterward, Bobby Joe would return and pick Rick up. When the tracks were "discovered," the photos of the mysterious beast— hopefully showing familiar landmarks on Burchfield's property— would appear on the news and catch the investors' attention.

That would be a game changer. So far, similar sightings had been written off as lies, pranks, or glimpses of bears or dogs. A confirmed report would throw a wrench into the already fragile gears of the construction-planning process, and would delay or kill any near-term commercialization. The casino industry was a risky business.

And Bobby Joe was probably right about Rick's sister Jenny. Even if she *did* know about Lorena's plan to sabotage Burchfield's project, Rick and Jenny hadn't been in touch since their mother died last month. Truth be known, Richard Harrelson was the black sheep of an otherwise respectable family. Goodhearted but lazy, Rick had failed at a range of endeavors—carpentry, auto repair, farming, even insurance. He was a disappointment to everyone he knew, including his wife Arlene. He made a mental note to call her if all this ran too long, tell her he'd be late.

His only friend in the world was Bobby Joe Faraday, and at times Rick wondered about *that* relationship. When Bobby Joe went to work for Gatewood Chemical last year, he turned weird. Still cocky, with his monogrammed hankies and the huge BJF JR engraved on his belt buckle, but brooding and distant. This was one of many confusing things in Rick's life these days.

But today's job would help. Nobody'd had to twist his arm— he'd just told Bobby Joe to point him where they wanted him to go. He'd been working all his life, and maybe this time, finally, things would go right. The thousand would tide him over until he could get his head straight and control his drinking and find honest work, even if it was just odd jobs around the county. If there was one thing he was good at, it was fixing things.

When Rick was suited up, the two men stood there a moment, staring at each other. The outfit really was scary. They shook hands, Bobby Joe looking even more uneasy than usual.

"By the way," Bobby Joe said, "what's a moralist?"

"The opposite of you and me," Rick said.

Bobby Joe nodded, and they parted company.

*

The first hundred yards was exhausting—not only because of the heavy suit and shoes but also because he had to stay in the soft bottomland to leave visible, wide-spaced footprints.

The heat inside the suit was worse than Rick had anticipated. He had to stop often and wipe the sweat from his eyes inside the hood. He wished he'd brought some water, though the sight of a hairy ape carrying a bottle of Aquafina might not be exactly what Madame Gatewood had in mind.

Twice he heard things moving in the woods, and he couldn't help hoping those creature sightings had been as false as most logical people assumed. He couldn't imagine a greater indignity than getting devoured by a real monster while doing this kind of cowardly playacting.

He'd trudged maybe half a mile when he saw the bend of the creek ahead, beyond which were the recognizable land features Bobby Joe wanted in his photos. The plan called for Rick to shuffle around in the trees with his back to the camera to hide the suit's buttons and the hood's eyeholes, while Bobby Joe snapped his pictures.

Puffing, Rick paused beneath a water oak, removed his left glove, and checked his watch. Two minutes to seven, which meant he was ahead of schedule. Even at this plodding rate, he'd be where he needed to be in fifteen minutes, and Bobby Joe was supposed to be in position at seven-thirty.

Rick was about to resume walking when his cell phone buzzed. Cursing, he struggled out of his glove again, pushed back his hood, sagged to the ground with his back against the tree, and fished out his phone. The display said JENNY HARRELSON.

Good old Jen. After a month of silence, his sister had to pick this moment to call.

"What is it?" he said.

"Well. What a sweet greeting."

"I'm a little busy. What's up?"

"I'm at your house, and nobody's home."

Rick blinked. "You're where?"

"I pounded on the door, and no one answered. After a while I got worried, and since I still have that key you gave me, I came in. Where are you, at seven on a Saturday morning?"

"Working." Rick didn't ask why she hadn't tried calling him *before* entering the house.

"Working where? And where's Arlene?"

"I'm out of town. Arlene must've gone shopping." Which she did often, lately. Just as well: his wife and sister hated each other. "What do you need?"

He could picture her rolling her eyes. "Your copy of Mom's death certificate. I guess I didn't make enough of 'em, and the bank wants one before letting me transfer Mom's IRA to the estate account. You still have that copy I gave you?"

"It's in the bedroom, metal box, bottom dresser drawer." He added, casually, "What do you hear about that casino your boss wants to build on Drowning Creek?"

Jenny snorted. "Sounds like you got some wrong info, little bro. Let's see ... bedroom, dresser, bottom drawer?" She paused. "Whoa—isn't that pretty!"

"What do you mean?"

"Nothing. Just something on the dresser."

"No, I mean what wrong info?" He could hear the creak of the drawer, the rustle of paper.

"The casino deal," she said. "It's dead, as of two days ago. Those creature sightings, false or not, scared the investors off."

Rick froze. "What?"

"Whoever called in those reports, or caused 'em, better hope Lorena never finds out who they are," Jenny said. "They cost her about twenty million dollars." He heard the drawer slide shut. "Got it. I'll make you another copy later."

"Wait a minute. How did those sightings cost *Lorena* money? They were on Walt Burchfield's land."

"Not anymore. It's Lorena's now. She bought him out last week. I figured your buddy Bobby Joe would've told you—he was with us when we drew up the papers."

Rick felt his stomach clench.

"I swear I can't stand that Bobby Joe Faraday," she said. "Richard? Are you there?"

He swallowed. "I gotta go, Jen."

"Are you all right? You sound—"

He disconnected and sat there, dumbstruck. His heart pounded inside the suit. Questions flashed through his mind like fireworks. This was *Gatewood* land, now?

Then why had Bobby Joe brought him here?

A chill ran up his backbone.

With trembling fingers, he punched in Jenny's number.

Please let me be wrong.

"Where are you?" he blurted, when she picked up.

"Back in the car. Why?"

"What was pretty?" he asked her.

"What?"

"You said you saw something on our dresser. Something pretty. What was it?"

Rick realized he was holding his breath.

"A button," Jenny said. "A pearl button."

He bowed his head, shut his eyes. Arlene didn't own anything with pearl buttons.

"Richard?"

He felt sick. He could hear his own voice, in Bobby Joe's truck an hour ago.

Looks like you lost one of your fancy buttons....

He understood all of it now. The lies, the secrecy, Bobby Joe's moodiness, Arlene's shopping trips.

The rifle and scope in the back seat of the truck.

"Richard? Say something."

He looked again at his watch. He had twenty-five minutes.

"I'll explain later. Keep your phone close, okay? And don't talk to anybody else."

"You're scaring me. What's going on?"

"I'm scared, too," he said.

*

Exactly thirty minutes later, Bobby Joe Faraday lowered his smoking 30.06 and stared at the woods on the far side of the creek. Nothing moved. Satisfied, he picked up his three empty shell casings, walked through the forest to his truck, and climbed in. This time, he kept the rifle up front. On the drive back, he stopped on the bridge and called the sheriff's office, using a lower voice and a drawly accent and a cheap phone he'd bought at Walmart.

His message was short and careful: "I'm reportin' shots fired along Drownin' Creek, about four miles northa the Highway Sixteen bridge. Where them sightin's was reported the other day. Three shots, sounded like a rifle. Right after that, a car come flyin' down that road westa the creek, musta been doin' eighty or ninety. Seemed funny to me, and since it ain't even deer season I figgered I'd let you folks know."

He tossed the phone off the bridge, followed by the rifle and shell casings. Damn shame—he'd had that gun a long time—but he'd been careful so far, might as well keep it up.

Lord, he felt good. He'd gambled and won. What was it they say? *Take me to the tables, roll me like the dice.*

His next call was made using his own phone. "Arlene? It's done. They'll contact you soon." He paused, listening, and felt himself grin. "Love you, too."

*

Jenny Harrelson poured two cups of coffee, took them out to her deck, set them on a table, and eased into a chair. She slid one of the steaming cups across the table and turned to look at her back yard. It was past nine and the sun had risen above the treetops, making her squint as she studied a fat crow perched on the homemade birdhouse near the fence. On the other side of the table, her brother Rick followed her gaze. The crow stared back at them.

"Doesn't look like he belongs here, does he?" Rick asked. "Kinda like me."

She smiled. "You belong here. You and I are the only family we have left."

Rick stayed quiet a moment, thinking about the past two hours.

"You going to tell me what happened?" Jenny said.

The crow flew away. They watched it fade into the distance. Rick took a sip of coffee. "What happened was, you saved my life today."

"By picking you up out there?"

"By calling me."

In a calm voice, he told her about the Bigfoot suit, the shoes, the money he'd been promised for the job, the fact that he thought he might finally have gotten lucky. He finished his tale with his discovery that Lorena wasn't involved in the scam but Bobby Joe and Arlene were.

Jenny nodded. "That clears things up," she said. "What do you think about the ... well, the part about Arlene?"

"What do *you* think?"

"I think they deserve each other."

He nodded. "You could be right."

A full minute passed.

"So what happened?" she asked. "Between our call and when I picked you up?"

"First tell me what you found out. What are the police saying?"

She took a breath, choosing her words. "My contact in the sheriff's office says they got an anonymous call a while ago, just after seven-thirty, from an unknown number—"

"Bobby Joe," Rick said.

"—informing them that rifle shots had been heard in the woods. When Sheriff Sims and one of his deputies checked it out around eight, they found some kind of bear or ape costume draped over a bush with three bullet holes in its back, along with matching gloves and giant fake footprints on the creek bank and two homemade shoe-thingies that must've made the tracks. It all indicated a prankster getting shot in mid-prank."

"Except there was no body."

"Right," she said. "No body, and nobody around to explain it. What I can't figure is why someone—"

"Bobby Joe."

"—why Bobby Joe would shoot an empty monster suit propped up motionless on a bush. Can you explain that?"

"Yes," he said. "It wasn't motionless."

"What?"

"That ball of twine I told you about? I still had it, in an inside pocket of the suit. After I draped the woolly coat on the bush, I tied the ends of several long pieces of twine to the suit and took the other ends with me to a hiding place back in the woods, out of sight. When I figured Bobby Joe was in position over there, I jerked on the lines every few seconds to make the suit move. He thought it was me and fired, three times. I stayed hidden for another ten minutes to give him time to pack up and leave, and then I phoned you to come rescue me and hiked out of the woods to the highway. And here we are."

For a long moment, neither of them spoke. A little sparrow was using the birdhouse now. He and Jenny watched it.

Finally, she spoke. "Is there anything at all in this that could lead the police back to you?"

"Only if they look hard enough. I probably left some of my hair inside the hood, and I sweated a river in that coat. But they won't test for DNA. There was no blood, nothing to suggest foul play, so there's no crime. They'll probably think a hoaxster got scared and left his disguise behind, and a hunter saw what looked like a wild animal and shot at it."

"Couldn't Bobby Joe tell 'em you were there?"

"Not without implicating himself for attempted murder."

Another silence.

"So that's it?" she asked. "Your best friend lies to you, steals your wife, tries to kill you, and it's over? He gets away clean?"

Rick smiled. "Not necessarily." He set his cup down. "Let me ask you a question. Who would you rather have mad at you and hunting for you—the law or Lorena Gatewood?"

"What kind of a question is that?"

"Answer me."

After a long pause, she said, "The law." She heaved a sigh. "Lorena's my client, and there are things I like about her. But I'm scared of her. And terrified of the people she employs."

He nodded. "I agree. Let's leave it at that. Everything's gonna be okay."

Surprisingly, she didn't argue. She just gave him a mysterious look and picked up the empty cups and took them inside.

Rick drew a deep breath and exhaled. He'd told his sister the truth. What he *hadn't* told her was that her contact in the sheriff's office hadn't given her a full report. Rick had left two objects in Bigfoot's pocket: the ball of twine and Bobby Joe's knife.

No evidence of a crime meant no arrest—but it didn't mean no one would be called in for questioning. The initials on the handle of the knife—BJF JR—would make it easy to find its owner. And when word about that got out, Ms. Gatewood would be especially interested.

As it turned out, nothing about this job had been easy. For him *or* Bobby Joe Faraday.

Jenny's voice snapped him out of his thoughts. "Want some breakfast?"

He hadn't realized he was hungry until now. "I could pay for it in labor," he said. "This deck could use some work."

"Sounds good to me." She leaned against the doorframe. "You know, depending on what happens with Arlene—"

"Yeah?"

"—you could move your stuff over here. Guest bedroom's empty."

They locked eyes.

"I might take you up on that," he said.

She looked thoughtful. "Actually—the shed and fence could use some work, too." Before he could reply, she grinned and ducked back into the kitchen.

When he focused again on the birdhouse, the sparrow poked its head out of the opening. As Rick watched, it looked around, apparently satisfied that it was home and safe.

Rick smiled. He knew the feeling.

The Bridge
Released July 1986

"Running on Ice"
"This Is the Time"
"A Matter of Trust"
"Modern Woman"
"Baby Grand"
"Big Man on Mulberry Street"
"Temptation"
"Code of Silence"
"Getting Closer"

All songs by Billy Joel
(except "Code of Silence" by Billy Joel and Cyndi Lauper).

A Matter of Trust
by David Dean

"Take a look at this," the lieutenant said, tossing a screen shot of a web page onto Sergeant Russell Turner's desk.

Picking it up, Russell studied the printout. It read:

SPOUSE REMOVAL SERVICES
When legal recourse no longer makes sense
or provides proper satisfaction.

There were two photos beneath the words. The one on the left showed a young man, smiling and carefree, striding through a crowded bar as slender women eyed him hungrily over the shoulders of their escorts. The second photo featured a good-looking woman driving a convertible, also sporting a smile, her blond hair flowing behind her, a young male model at her side, gazing at her profile in rapt adoration, the road ahead undulating toward a beautiful sunset above a dramatic coastline.

Along the bottom of the page was printed an email address.

Russell had little doubt that both photos had been "shopped" from glossy ads that had nothing to do with *spouseremoval-services.com*.

"Is this serious?" he asked, offering the printout back to the lieutenant, who stood over him, muscular forearms exposed by his rolled-up sleeves, handsome face composed as always. "It's a joke, right?"

But it did not appear as if Lieutenant Steven Wallace agreed, his easy smile vanishing like something best forgotten. "That's for you to determine, Russ—your *job*, last time I looked."

Doesn't even bother to call me sergeant, Russell thought. *He knows an inferior when he sees one.*

He tried again, slapping the paper with three pudgy fingers. "It's got to be a joke, L T. Nobody in their right mind would advertise something like this." A lock of his dark hair slipped down his forehead. In brushing it away, he managed to knock his glasses askew.

The lieutenant looked on as if witnessing something sad. "You too busy, Russ?"

This was a trick question: Russell's boss knew exactly how little he was working on at the moment. "How did you come across this, anyway?" he asked, trying to salvage a little dignity.

Lowering his lean rump onto the edge of Russell's desk, the younger man explained, "A patrolman was given it yesterday at a coffee shop, owner says he found it tacked to their corkboard. Didn't know who put it there and hadn't given anyone permission to do so. He didn't like the looks of it, so we—no, *you've* got it. Check it out, and get back to me if it's anything."

The lieutenant strode out of the detective bureau's cybercrime unit—which consisted solely of Sergeant Russell Turner—without another word.

Taking a deep breath, Russell gazed round the small institutional-green office he occupied in the basement of Wessex Township's police department. Besides his cluttered desk and computer, there was little to see. The only window was at ground level and covered with heavy wire mesh. His view of the outside world was of his fellow officers' shoes and boots passing on their way to their more robust tasks of patrolling the streets, making arrests, effecting rescues.

The only decoration in the room was a photo of him and Claire on their honeymoon eight years before—she honey-haired and clad in a white two-piece bathing suit, smiling indolently at the camera, he, a much trimmer version of his present self, also in a bathing suit, tanned and confident.

He had been a patrol officer then and up for promotion. The world had been spread out before him, and he had been happy and in love. Claire had been—and still was—everything that mattered most in his world.

Then it had all gone wrong. A routine stop on a car drifting in and out of its lane, a kid so nervous his hands were trembling when he passed Russell a driver's license not two days old. Taking pity on him, Russell issued a mild warning and welcomed the lad to the driving world. Returning to his patrol car, he couldn't hear the boy's vehicle over the roar of passing traffic.

The teenager—still shaken by the encounter—inadvertently placed his car in reverse and gunned the accelerator to merge. Russell was struck down, his left leg run over. He remembered nothing more until he came to in the ER, too groggy from painkillers to appreciate how bad the damage was. In the end, he kept the leg, but he would never be able to walk without difficulty. His days of active police work were over.

Thanks to his stellar record and a benign police chief, he was retrained for the newly instituted cybercrime position—and, three years later, there he remained, softening into a man he barely recognized ... a man who devoted hours to the contemplation of the deaths of his wife and her new, unknown lover. Given those unspoken thoughts, this flyer for "Spouse Removal Services" seemed to him a cruel cosmic joke.

His suspicions had begun at the Christmas party Claire's boss threw each year. He drank too much, and they had a tiff over it. At some point, he lost track of her.

Later, making his way through the crowded banquet hall rented for the occasion, he caught a glimpse of Claire standing near the coat racks, almost hidden by the winter garments clustered against the wall. Leaning back against someone's fur coat, she was sheathed in a sleeveless red dress that ended mid-thigh, her white teeth bared in a glistening smile.

Concealed within the deeper shadows of the alcove was another figure, a tall male in a dark suit. Russell couldn't see his face, but he appeared to be stroking Claire's hip.

He hurried toward them, his hobble aggravated by the exertion, and arrived flushed and sweating to find Claire alone.

"Who was that?" he demanded, his slur pronounced even to his own ears. "He had his hands on you!"

Out of the corner of his eye, he saw the exit door closing.

"I have no idea, Russ. Somebody's husband or boyfriend, I guess. He was as drunk as you are and stopped to wish me a Merry Christmas on his way home."

She handed him his coat, snagging the car keys from the side pocket. "I'll drive," she announced.

After that evening, Claire's job—which had seldom before required her to travel or work weekends—suddenly began demanding both on a regular basis.

He knew she must be having an affair.

The grief of loss and betrayal weighed on Russell's heart like a stone, but he was so fearful of what might happen if he confronted her that he didn't push the matter further. He couldn't decide which was worse, facing a moment of truth that, once revealed, could never be forgotten, or trudging along in willful half-ignorance, the poisonous seed of jealousy growing within him like a cancer.

He shook off these unhappy thoughts and typed the URL from the bottom of the flyer into his browser.

"I'll be damned," he murmured, as the page loaded.

On the screen appeared a velvety royal-blue background with ornate lettering reminiscent of a Victorian funeral announcement.

Russell selected the "About Us" tab and clicked on it. Against the same background as the home page, a block of text appeared:

> *It is a sad statement of our times that divorce has become commonplace. Yet as necessary as the ending of a marriage may be under some circumstances, the usual handling of such a wrenching decision is unsatisfactory to many people. If you are reading this page, you may be—and probably are—one of those people.*
>
> *For you, the matter is anything but a routine legal action to be undertaken by unfeeling lawyers. Instead, it is something far more significant. The issue is not just freedom from an unhappy*

marriage, but freedom from a person who has caused you great sorrow.

In some cases—yours, perhaps—divorce will not provide proper satisfaction and meaningful resolution. Something more is called for, and that something is what we at Spouse Removal Services provide: the ultimate state of control, marriage dissolution, relationship erasure, true and complete closure.

In addition to the emotional rewards provided by such a service, there are other benefits to being divested completely of an unhealthy relationship. Consider, for example, the long-term financial stability achieved when all costs associated with the end of a damaging entanglement can be eliminated after only two payments.

If what has been described here sounds as if it might be of interest, please contact us at....

"This is a joke," Russell said aloud to the empty room. "It has to be a joke. You'd have to be crazy...."

The sentence trailed off.

On the screen, his cursor winked on the email link.

He thought of Claire in the arms of another man.

A car horn and the slamming of doors jarred him from his trance. Muffled voices and the scuffle of footsteps passed his basement window, reminding him that it was four o'clock and shift change. Shutting down his computer, he rose, slipped on his coat, and limped out, locking the office door behind him.

*

Two hours later, Russell received a text from Claire: "Jill got engaged last night! Impromptu office party for her after work. Okay?"

Putting his beer down, Russell pecked a question onto the tiny screen: "Where? Maybe I'll join you."

After a long wait, his phone dinged with a reply: "Not decided yet but it's all girls. Sorry!"

"Have fun," he answered.

She had made the mistake several weeks before of giving him the name of a restaurant where she and "the girls" were supposedly celebrating another impromptu occasion. He'd stopped in unannounced, but neither she nor her fellow workers were there. When he questioned her, later that night, she looked him in the eye and said, "It was too crowded, so we went somewhere else."

When did she become so cold? Russell asked himself. She had always been such a happy, emotional girl. Now, he hardly knew her.

Rising, he hobbled into the kitchen and poured himself a generous shot of bourbon. Bringing the tumbler to his lips, he saw that the amber liquid was trembling and set it down, spilling some onto his hand.

"Goddammit, Claire," he whispered, a tear running down his cheek, "I don't deserve this."

*

Russell entered his office the next morning with the dull throb of a hangover pulsing in his skull. His wavy hair was tousled, his eyes bloodshot. Flopping down at his desk, he flicked on the computer, removed the lid from the cup of coffee he had bought on the way in, and took a sip.

Claire had come home after midnight. After taking a furtive shower in the guest bathroom, she slipped beneath the sheets of their bed with the hiss of flesh against fabric. Moments later, she was breathing deeply.

Despite everything, he felt a deep longing for her. It had been three months since they had last made love, and he missed her touch even more than the sex itself.

He slept fitfully, woke long before Claire, rose, dressed, and left the house. He was thirty minutes early for work.

With dull resolve, he surfed to *spouseremovalservices.com*, clicked the email link, and typed, "Interested in your service. What next?"

He understood that he was taking a great risk in using a police computer but reasoned that he had a perfect alibi. After all, hadn't Lieutenant Wallace assigned him the task of investigating the site? *If* anything came of it, and *if* things went awry, he could fashion an explanation: a sting gone terribly wrong.

He stared at the screen for several minutes, waiting, then closed the browser. Rising, he limped to the men's room, feeling as if a void had opened within him. His stomach clenched in sympathy, like a fist around a bird.

The men's room was empty. He staggered to the nearest stall and vomited.

*

When Russell returned to his office, he found a response to his email waiting: a telephone number and the words "3 PM." Nothing more.

He stared at the message. *It's not too late to back away*, he told himself.

He opened a case file—an unsolved series of threats and cyber-stalking—and studied it, but his thoughts kept returning to Spouse Removal. Though common sense and long experience told him the "service" was most likely a hoax or scam, he couldn't deny that he was curious.

With a *frisson* of terror, it occurred to him that the site could have been designed by the Feds, a way of trolling the net for would-be murderers. Perspiration broke out on his skin at the thought.

Still, he had been assigned to look into the site, and he was committing no crime by doing so. Not yet.

He forced himself to concentrate on the stalking case, and the hours shambled on toward three.

*

His call was answered by an automated message that advised him to leave a number and promised he would be contacted as soon as possible.

Russell paused, the moment made anticlimactic by the mundanity of the robotic voice, and then he gave his personal cell number and disconnected, his palms sweating.

He had crossed a line—an invisible line the nuns had warned him about, the line his instructors at the police academy had assured him a cop treads close to every day but should never, *ever* cross.

His cell phone rang. The words "Caller Unknown" appeared on the screen. His heart pounding, Russell answered.

"Yes?"

There was a crackling noise, like signal interference. "You called us," an electronically modulated voice replied. Russell couldn't tell if it was a man or a woman on the line.

"Yes, I did," he said.

"And you are?"

"Steve," he lied, giving his boss's name. "Steven Wallace."

"That's not the name registered to the phone you're using," the tinny voice informed him. "You are Russell Turner. Is that correct?"

"Yes," Russell admitted, feeling foolish and a little frightened. His phone's settings should have prevented his name from coming up for an unknown caller. "Who are you?"

"I am with Spouse Removal Services. That's all you need to know, Russell. It's better for both of us, this way." The words warped and woofed, the voice didn't even sound human. "What is it you want from us?"

"You know what I want," Russell answered, piqued by the question and the casual use of his name.

"Say it aloud."

He felt his annoyance grow far out of proportion to the situation.

"What do you think I want? What does anybody want when they call you?"

"Say it."

"Spouse removal, goddammit! Are you happy?"

"Thank you."

"You're recording this, aren't you?" Russell challenged. He did the same thing in his own investigations.

"She's hurt you, hasn't she? I can hear it. Do I presume too much when I say *she*?"

Russell felt himself sag. "No. Her name is ... Claire."

There was no going back now.

"Can I safely assume she's taken a lover—broken her marriage vows? Would that be correct?"

"What difference does it make?" Russell answered, his earlier anger giving way to sadness and shame.

"We promise *complete* resolution, Russell. In cases like yours, where the client is so obviously suffering—as opposed to those cases driven only by cold financial concerns—we would be happy to include the other party for half our usual charge."

"He might be married," Russell heard himself saying, "might have children. I couldn't live with that."

"Do *you*?"

"Have children? No ... no, we don't."

"That makes things easier, doesn't it?"

Russell thought the voice was clearer now, less modulated, almost human.

"How much?" he asked, his own voice drained of emotion.

"Fifty thousand dollars—twenty-five up front, the rest once the dissolution has been completed. Is that acceptable?"

"It's a lot of money—I can't come up with that kind of cash without Claire finding out about it."

"You shouldn't worry about that, Russell. Once the down payment is received, things will move rather quickly. You'll see."

"Will she be hurt?"

"Do you care?"

"Yes."

"Then no, I can promise you that she won't be hurt."

Russell wondered about the use of "I" language. "Do you work alone?" he asked.

"No questions of that nature, please. Since you are a police officer, the less you know the better."

"How do you—?" Russell began, then caught himself.

"I've run quite a thorough background check on you, Russell," the voice explained.

"Then how do you know this isn't a trap?"

"I *understand* you, Russell—your life, your love, your hurt—and I believe I can trust you. When all's been said and done, it boils down to a matter of trust, doesn't it? You know that better than I— having suffered the loss of it. It may comfort you to know that you're not the first law-enforcement officer I've assisted. Now, as to the money, it's to be transferred electronically to the following account—are you prepared to write it down?"

Russell scribbled the information onto a pad.

"If questioned, you can say you're investing in Timmons and Westlake Financial Ventures. Payment within forty-eight hours, please. You'll be—"

"Forty-eight hours!" Russell erupted. "I can't—"

The call abruptly disconnected, and Russell sat there with his silent cell phone in his hand.

"Any progress on that spouse-removal thing?"

He spun around to find Lieutenant Wallace leaning into his office from the corridor.

"No," he stammered, wondering how long the man had been standing there. "Not yet. I sent them an email and got a number to call, but no one picked up." He forced his pulse to slow. "I think some kid must have put it up as a hoax."

"How about the website itself? Anything there—graphic photos, threats?"

"Nothing explicit. It's all pretty vague, actually."

"All right, then. Keep me posted if anything develops."

"Of course," Russell answered to an empty doorway. The lieutenant had already gone off to attend to other, more important matters.

*

At lunchtime, he drove to Claire's office. He wasn't sure why, but he suddenly had the urge to see her. In spite of what he had just done—perhaps *because* of it—he was overcome with a sudden tenderness for the person he had fallen in love with and married.

He was greeted by one of her co-workers, a young woman with a dark complexion and long shining hair. He thought she was called Rita.

"Hi, Russ," she waved. "You just missed Claire."

"Did I? I didn't think she'd take off for lunch *this* early. I was going to surprise her."

"That's sweet, but she had a doctor's appointment and said she wouldn't be back. Did you forget?"

Russell felt his face coloring, but not for the reason Rita might think—he wasn't embarrassed at forgetting something he'd never been told.

"Oh, right." He managed a smile. "She mentioned it at breakfast—I *did* forget."

"My husband would've, too," she assured him.

Nodding, Russell turned for the exit. He wondered if Rita knew what Claire was up to. Maybe the entire office did. Since he'd been at the Christmas party, her mystery man was almost certainly one of her co-workers—or one of their husbands.

He drove straight to his bank and transferred the money to the numbered account.

*

When Claire arrived home, Russell was on his third drink. "Went ahead and ate," he announced, a little too loudly.

"Am I that late?" she murmured. "I should've called."

"I'm used to it," he replied, studying her distracted expression.

She sat on the sofa, almost within touching distance.

"Did you get something to eat?" she asked.

"I just *said* I did," Russell growled. "You should've had your *doctor* test your hearing."

Claire's head snapped up. "I felt like I was coming down with something—she said I'm run down and should get more iron."

"That's a lie, Claire, and you know it."

Before she could respond to his accusation, his phone rang. The screen read: "Caller Unknown."

"It's work," he said, and headed for the bedroom.

"When did you start using your own phone for work?" Claire demanded, as he shut the door behind him.

"We have the money," the mechanized voice crackled in his ear. "Thank you. That was prompt."

"What now?"

"Does your wife leave for work before or after you do?"

"After. I leave around seven-thirty, but she doesn't have to be in until nine."

"You're scheduled to work tomorrow?"

"Yes."

"Good. Go to work at your normal time."

Despite his hurt and anger, Russell felt a moment of doubt. This was going to happen.

"Tomorrow? That seems so—"

"It's like ripping off a Band-Aid, Russell. Best to do it quickly."

"Do I—?"

"Just come home after your shift, as usual."

"Yeah, but what'll—"

The line buzzed.

When Russell returned to the living room, he found it empty. He could hear the shower running in the master bath. For one crazy moment, he thought of joining his wife there, surprising her, as he had done in the earliest days of their marriage, when such things had been spontaneous and joyful.

Then, recalling where she'd been and what he'd set in motion, he stalked into the kitchen and downed another shot of bourbon.

*

The following day was an agony of waiting in his cell of an office. Unable to concentrate on any one thing, Russell was only vaguely aware of the comings and goings of his fellow officers in the parking lot. Overly warm one moment, he grew suddenly cold and clammy the next. The only thing he could think of was what was going to happen—might in fact already have happened—to Claire. The hands on the wall clock appeared to have stopped altogether, then jumped forward whenever he managed to distract himself for what seemed only moments.

It was almost lunch time when the lieutenant threw open his door and leaned in. "Anything on that—what was it called, again?"

"Spouse Removal Services," Russell managed to answer over the blood pumping like thunder in his ears.

"Yeah, that. Nothing?"

"Nothing," Russell echoed.

"Gonna write it up, Russ? Give me something to close out?"

"Yeah, sure, I was just getting started."

Crossing his arms, Wallace leaned against the doorframe and asked, "What's wrong with you?"

"What do you mean?"

"You don't look well. You're kinda pale. You sick?"

"I'm fine. Some indigestion, maybe."

The lieutenant appeared unconvinced. "Go home if you're sick, Russell," he said, without the slightest note of sympathy in his voice.

Home, Russell thought.

*

When he pulled into the driveway, he saw Claire's car in the garage. It was half past four, and she almost never got back from work before six.

Russell climbed out of his car on wobbly legs, the damaged one feeling as if it might give way altogether. The door connecting the garage to the mudroom was locked.

He fumbled his key into the slot. Stepping into the house, he stopped and listened. All he could hear was the soft rush of heated air through the floor vents.

It occurred to him that Spouse Removal Services might still be on the premises. That he—or she, or they—might be waiting for him, either to demand the second payment or, just as likely, to kill him, too ... or *instead*. Perhaps they'd allowed Claire to pay them to switch their attentions from her to him.

He drew his gun and eased his way down the hall.

The pistol held out before him, he stepped around the dividing wall and into the living room.

Claire sat silently on the sofa, her eyes widening at the sight of him, then filling with hate.

Something cold and metallic touched the skin where his neck met the back of his skull, and a familiar voice said, "Lay it on the carpet, Russ, and don't make any sudden moves, okay?"

Russell did as he was told.

Claire stormed across the room and slapped him hard across the face. "You sick bastard!" she hissed. "Steve told me everything!"

His face stinging, Russell thought, *Steve....*

"Sit down, honey," Steven Wallace told Claire. She did so, and the lieutenant took a step back, his own gun aimed at Russell's heart.

"*You're* Spouse Removal Services?" Russell asked.

"Hardly," Steve replied. "Spouse Removal Services is a pimply twenty-six-year-old kid, who is crying his little eyes out as we speak. He's apparently pulled this scam off several times already. Never actually killed anyone, of course—that would've required him to leave his parents' cozy basement. None of his 'clients' ever complained—but how could they, after commissioning him to commit a murder?"

"But—"

"I heard enough of your side of the conversation yesterday to realize you were up to no good. When I confirmed that you were using your private phone to communicate with the target of an investigation, I called in a little outside help from the State. It was easy from there."

"You and Claire...?"

"Since Christmas."

Russ remembered the silhouette of a tall man stroking his wife's hip. "So now what? I go to prison?"

"That's the way I see it."

"You've got it all figured out."

"You handed it to us, Russ."

"There's just one thing," Russell said, feeling a resolve he had not felt for a very long time.

"Oh?"

"I'm gonna go for my gun ... and if you don't kill me first, I'm gonna kill you." Glancing at Claire, whose expression had gone from fury to fear, he added, "Her, too."

"Don't be an idiot, Russ! You'll be dead before you can get to it—and it'll be a justified shooting, you know that."

"Will it? The DA's office will have to investigate, and *everything* will come out. Once they know about you and Claire, I wonder how the Grand Jury will rule. Any guesses, Steve?"

The uncertainty on his wife's and her lover's faces were all he could have hoped for.

Russell Turner took a slow breath. "The kid at Spouse Removal Services was wrong," he said. "It *never* was a matter of trust."

And with those words he reached for his gun.

Storm Front

Released October 1989

"That's Not Her Style"
"We Didn't Start the Fire"
"The Downeaster 'Alexa'"
"I Go to Extremes"
"Shameless"
"Storm Front"
"Leningrad"
"State of Grace"
"When in Rome"
"And So It Goes"

All songs by Billy Joel.

The Downeaster 'Alexa'
by Michael Bracken

"Where are the fucking fish?" Joel Williams pounded the flat of his hand against the worn wood of the bar. Captain of the Downeaster *Alexa II*, he'd stopped for a beer at the Sand Bar instead of going directly home. "I know they're out there. They have to be."

Karl Winestadt, captain of the *Georgina*, which had docked only a few hours before the *Alexa II*, straddled the stool to Joel's left. A hearty, broad-chested man with a mane of blond hair, he was several beers ahead of the younger captain.

"I've been to Block, Alvin, Atlantis, and Veatch," Joel said, naming four of the thirty-five major undersea canyons lining the continental shelf from the Canadian boundary down to Cape Hatteras in North Carolina. Upwellings of cold water around the steep-walled canyons brought nutrients that traditionally supported a food chain of ever-larger sea life from plankton to finback whales and included the bluefin tuna and swordfish that provided his primary income. "I just can't find 'em."

"We're all in the same boat," Karl commiserated. "The waters around here ain't what they used to be, not like when my daddy and your granddaddy were reeling them in as fast as they could drop a hook."

Joel motioned to the bartender. "Give me another."

Eddie Shumway limped the length of the bar, his prosthetic leg no longer cooperating. A bald, leather-faced man well into his eighties, he had worked the stick at the Sand Bar since shortly after the accident that had ended his fishing career. "You'll have to pay for the first one, first."

"Put it on my tab," Joel said.

"Can't do that. The new owner—"

"New owner? When did this place get a new owner?"

"Two weeks ago," Eddie said. "New owner gave me three months to clear up everybody's tabs. Anything that ain't been paid by then comes out of my last paycheck. After that, they're shutting the place down for a remodel."

Joel looked around at the unpainted shiplap walls covered with nautical paraphernalia, most of which had not changed or been dusted since the days when his grandfather had commandeered the stool upon which he sat. "What's to remodel?"

"Probably going to turn the place into a Red Lobster," Karl said, "or a wine bar."

Joel pushed himself up, dug in his pocket for change, and paid for his lone beer.

"Remora's been looking for you," Eddie said. Ruben "Remora" Ramirez collected debts for a loan shark named Buddy Fineman. "If you have to work that hard to dredge up the price of a beer, this might not be the best time to run into him."

Joel agreed. He dug again for his key ring and found his twenty-year-old Ford F-250 in the parking lot outside.

He drove south on West Lake, on his way to the three-bedroom, two-bath house on Essex where he had grown up. In the distance, Joel could see the multimillion-dollar monstrosity a part-time resident had built on the lot where he and his wife Jennifer had once owned a home. They had used money his mother had saved from his father's life-insurance payout to put a down payment on the *Alexa II* and on that home, and for several years they had been happy there. When things began turning sour, he had sold the house despite his wife's wishes and used what little profit he made to pay down the debt on the boat. He and his family—Jennifer, daughter Maria, and son Tommy—had moved back into his childhood home with his mother.

His mother and children were asleep when he arrived, but he found his wife sitting in the kitchen, nursing a cup of decaf laced with cheap whiskey from a half-empty bottle. She looked up. "How'd you do?"

Joel shook his head. "Not good. Barely covered expenses."

"There's a job open at the insurance company," Jennifer said.

"I'm not working for the damn insurance company." Joel sat opposite his wife. "My father was born a bayman, and he died a bayman."

"But you don't have to." When he didn't respond, she continued. "Joel, please. At least consider what I'm suggesting. Imagine what a job with a steady paycheck would—"

"My father's father and his father before him were baymen, and so were all the men back more generations than I have fingers to count on. It's who we are."

"Not my son," Jennifer said. "He's not swimming in his daddy's wake. Not like you did."

Joel glared at her.

"Tommy's had a growth spurt," she said. "His pants are too short, and his shoes are pinching his toes."

"I'll figure something out."

Jennifer finished her whiskey-laced decaf and made her way to bed, leaving Joel alone in the kitchen staring through the living room at the oversized wood-framed photo hung above the fireplace mantel. In the grainy black-and-white image taken long before Joel's birth, his father stood on the dock next to his *Alexa*, and there had never been a day since his birth when that photograph had not determined Joel's fate.

In third grade, he had learned about a mythical lost island, and that's what he first thought of when his mother sat him on the living-room couch and told him his father was trolling Atlantis. His father and Eddie Shumway had been fishing a deep undersea canyon when a rogue wave capsized the *Alexa*, and only Eddie had survived. The story he told the insurance investigators grew with each retelling—like the stories fishermen tell of the one that got away—but Eddie attributed his survival to the actions Joel's father had taken as the *Alexa* succumbed to that rogue wave, though the leg he lost that night ensured he would never again crew a Downeaster.

Joel switched off the light, grabbed the bottle his wife had left behind, and drank in the darkness, unable to live up to his father's legacy.

*

His mother found him there in the kitchen the next morning.

"Get up, Joel," the wiry little woman said, poking him in the ribs. "You don't want your children to see you like this."

Joel blinked, straightened, used his top incisors to scrape the scum from his tongue. His son was already stirring on the couch, and he could hear his daughter in the bathroom.

"You need to think about your family," his mother continued, "not your pride."

"But—"

"You're not your father," she said. "You never will be."

The Baymen's Bank & Trust president had told him as much three years earlier when he'd requested an extension on his loan. Between his daughter's need for braces, the rebuilt transmission for Jennifer's minivan, and the increased cost of traveling deeper into the Atlantic to find fish, he had tapped out their savings.

"We can't loan you any more money, Joel," the banker said.

"But you've known me my entire life. Me and your boy went to school together. You knew my daddy. You know I'm good for it."

"I know your father would be good for it," the banker said, "but I'm sorry, it doesn't matter what I think. Our loan decisions are now made in New York."

He stood and extended his hand.

Joel didn't take it. Instead, he rose and stormed out of the office.

As the door closed behind him, the bank president raised his voice: "The next time you come in, ask to see your loan officer."

Over beer at the Sand Bar that evening, Joel had complained of his treatment at Baymen's Bank & Trust and learned he wasn't the only boat captain to get short shrift. He also learned of an alternative financing option—Buddy Fineman—and that option had been causing him further distress ever since.

Joel's mother poked him again. "Throw away that bottle and get out of my kitchen, so I can make breakfast."

Joel rose and buried the whiskey bottle in the trash bin beneath the sink. Then he made his way to his childhood bedroom and found Jennifer half-dressed.

As she stuffed her arms into a blue chambray shirt, she said, "You never came to bed."

"I—"

A stack of papers atop his wife's dresser caught his attention, and he stepped past her to examine them. He and Jennifer had dated throughout high school, had married only weeks after graduation, and had weathered many storms together. Now another storm seemed to be brewing. He turned to her, a fistful of overdue notices in his hand. "This why you're upset?"

"It isn't you," she said. "It's what's happening to us, what's happening to everyone like us. I don't want our children to go through what we're going through."

"I'll figure something out."

"I know you will," Jennifer said. "You always do."

She wrapped her hands around the back of his neck, pulled his face down, and kissed him. A moment later, she drew back and made a face. "God, you taste terrible."

Then she kissed him again.

*

Paying off Buddy Fineman's loan had proven impossible, but avoiding Ruben "Remora" Ramirez was a little easier. Joel took the *Alexa II* out twice before Remora caught up to him one evening. When he came up on deck after installing a new bilge pump, he found the big man waiting for him.

Though Joel stood an even six feet tall and had blue-collar muscles, the kind built from hard physical labor, Remora towered over him. Fineman's goon was not, however, familiar with the rhythms of a ship, even one at dock, and he swayed in a way that Joel did not.

"You're late," Remora said.

Joel wiped his hands on a rag and tossed it aside. "I've been working," he said. "The fish don't catch themselves."

"Too bad," Remora said. "That would make everyone's life much easier."

They stared at one another, and Joel realized how alone he was. Though he could see the lights of the Sand Bar several hundred yards away, no one else seemed to be on the dock or in any of the nearby Downeasters.

"I haven't got it," he finally admitted.

Remora shook his head. "That won't make Mr. Fineman happy."

"Don't tell him."

"You think you're a funny man," Remora said, balling his fists, "but you aren't the first person to tell me that joke, and you leave me to provide the punch line."

Joel had survived several fistfights as a teenager and a pair of bar fights in his twenties, but he had never faced a man who made his living intimidating others. He said, "You don't have to do this."

"Oh, but I do," Remora said. "If I do not make a lesson out of you, Mr. Fineman will make a lesson out of me."

He stepped forward, threw a left jab and followed it with a right cross, but the motion of the *Alexa II* broke his rhythm. The punches missed Joel's face, and he put up his fists to protect himself as he stepped backward.

Remora followed with a left hook that caught him in the breadbasket.

Joel took another step, and his hand bumped a gaff—the long hooked pole used to stab and lift large fish into the boat. Instinctively, he swung it upward, aiming for where the collection agent would have gills were he a bluefin tuna. The hook caught the big man under the chin and came out through his left eye, severing his carotid artery and puncturing his brain.

Remora fell to the deck and was trolling Atlantis before Joel realized the big man was dead. He dropped the gaff, leaned over the rail, and voided his dinner into the bay.

When he realized no one had seen what had happened, he pulled on work gloves and emptied Remora's pockets. He found a key ring sporting a dozen keys and a Chevrolet fob; an assortment of small change; a wallet containing the dead man's I.D., credit cards, folding money, and little else; a small black notebook with debtors identified by code along with a record of their payments; and several thousand dollars in cash, mostly Benjamins. He pocketed the keys, the cash, and the debt book and returned everything else to the dead man's pockets.

Then he wrestled the gaff hook out of Remora's head, sealed the body in an insulated bag usually used for fresh-caught tuna, and dragged it below deck where it could not be seen.

Joel hosed off the deck and went in search of a Chevrolet that would respond to Remora's key fob. He found a black Equinox parked behind the Sand Bar that unlocked at the fob's command, and he searched it, discovering another eight thousand dollars in cash in the center console and a semi-automatic pistol in a holster strapped beneath the driver's seat. Certain that no one had seen him, Joel drove the Equinox half a mile away and parked it at one of the motels facing the Block Island Sound, where it might not be noticed for several days.

He took the currency, left the pistol, and walked back to the dock's parking lot, where he'd left his F-250 earlier that day. On the way home, he stopped long enough to separate the smaller bills from the Benjamins. He dug through the glove compartment for his emergency flashlight, removed the D batteries, replaced them with the rolled-up hundred-dollar bills and Remora's keys, tossed the batteries out the window, and returned the flashlight and the notebook to the glove compartment.

At home, he left the smaller bills atop his wife's dresser, showered, and slipped into bed beside her.

*

Jennifer woke him several hours later. She had a fistful of wrinkled currency in her hand, and she pushed it in his face. "Where did this come from?"

"I sold some old gear," Joel said, with a smile he hoped looked genuine. "Pay some bills, buy Tommy some new clothes."

"I will," his wife said. "I'll take him shopping after school."

"Get Maria something, too," Joel added. His daughter had stopped growing, but fashion hadn't stopped changing.

Jennifer leaned down and kissed his forehead. "I knew you'd come through," she said. "You always do."

*

There was a dead body in a bag in the hold of Joel's Downeaster, and it wouldn't disappear on its own. Taking Remora out to sea and dumping him overboard was the obvious solution, but if sharks didn't tear the corpse apart and it floated back to shore, there was a chance it could be traced to him.

He had several things to do that morning, so he rolled out of bed and showered.

"Your wife had a smile on her face," his mother said, when he joined her in the kitchen. By then the kids had left for school, and Jennifer had gone to her part-time job at the 7-Eleven. "I'm guessing you won the lottery."

"I sold some old gear," he told her, repeating the lie.

His mother stared hard at him, and Joel knew she didn't believe his story. Even so, she didn't challenge him. "You want breakfast?"

"Not this morning." He glanced at the photograph of his father hanging above the fireplace mantel and realized for the first time in his life that his fate was in his own hands. "I have things to do."

He drove to East Hampton, Bridgehampton, and Sag Harbor, making several stops along the way, and when he returned to the

Alexa II late that afternoon, his flashlight was several Benjamins lighter.

Nothing had changed on his boat: Remora's body remained untouched.

He needed a drink, so he walked over to the Sand Bar, straddled his grandfather's stool, and ordered a beer.

"Can you pay for it?" Eddie asked.

Joel tossed a twenty on the bar and said, "Keep bringing them until this runs out."

Eddie limped away and returned with a mug filled from the tap.

Karl Winestadt was sitting with several other captains at a table on the far side of the bar. He left them, settled onto a stool next to Joel, and said, "Fineman's been around. He says his goon didn't turn in this week's collections. That means seven debtors have missed a payment. They'll have to pay double next month if Remora doesn't surface soon. I'm one of them."

"That isn't right," Joel said. "If you paid, you paid. It isn't your fault Fineman has unreliable help."

"What about you?"

"Never saw him."

"So you still owe this month's vig?"

Joel hesitated for a moment, realizing what he'd just implied. "I suppose I do."

"Then you're one of the lucky ones," Karl said. "If you've got it to pay. The rest of us are going to be hard-pressed to pay double next month. We had a tough enough time coming up with the vig for this month."

"It's the fucking fish," Joel said, raising his mug.

"It's the fucking fish," Karl agreed, raising his.

After Karl returned to his table, Eddie refilled Joel's mug and said, "Too bad your father's not here."

"Why's that?"

"He would know what to do." The bartender nodded at the other captains. "He'd find a way to toss those boys a lifeline. If it wasn't for him, I wouldn't be here now."

"Give it a rest," Joel said. "You've been milking that story since I was a fry."

Eddie looked hard at Joel. "It was him or me," he said. "We couldn't both cling to that buoy."

Joel finished his beer, told Eddie to keep the change, and drove home.

Both children were asleep—Maria in her room, Tommy on the couch—but his mother and wife were sitting at the kitchen table. "A Mr. Fineman phoned for you," Jennifer said. "He said you have a financial matter to discuss, and he wants to see you at his place tomorrow. He didn't sound like he was from the bank."

"Buddy Fineman's got his hooks in half the baymen on this end of the island," his mother said. "Just like the baymen, his family's been passing that business from generation to generation, but he's the last of his bloodline."

Jennifer asked, "What have you gotten yourself into?"

"Nothing I can't get myself out of," Joel assured her.

The look on his mother's face suggested her skepticism, but when she folded her arms over her chest and said nothing, Joel took his wife's hand and led her to the bedroom for the first time in months.

*

He slept well, was the first up the next morning, and had breakfast with his children before they set off for school. He left home the same time as his wife, and they headed in different directions.

The *Georgina* was gone from her slip by the time Joel arrived at the *Alexa II*. He spent the morning preparing for his meeting with Buddy Fineman. Late that afternoon, he took three thousand dollars from his flashlight, put it in a #10 envelope, and stuffed the envelope in his shirt pocket. He left his F-250 parked at the Montauk train station, retrieved Remora's Equinox from the motel parking lot, and drove to Buddy Fineman's home on the far side of Lake Montauk. Fineman answered his knock.

"I expected to see you before now."

Joel tapped the envelope jutting from his pocket. "I came as soon as I could."

Fineman looked past Joel at the Equinox, then stepped aside and let Joel into his foyer, a space nearly as large as the home Joel's family shared with his mother. Fineman led Joel through a set of double doors into an office and settled into a leather chair behind a walnut desk big enough for a game of table tennis. He did not offer Joel a seat.

"I heard your wife took your boy shopping for new clothes. Also heard you paid your insurance premiums with cash. Where'd you get the money?"

"Where'd you hear all that?"

"A man tossing hundred-dollar bills around doesn't go unnoticed. Where," Fineman repeated, "did you get the money?"

"I sold some old gear."

"To whom? No one around here has—"

"Out-of-towner," Joel said, growing more comfortable with his lie. He tossed the envelope containing three thousand dollars onto Fineman's desk.

"Why not pay Ruben?" Fineman didn't use his collector's nickname.

"Never saw him," Joel said. "That's why I brought this directly to you."

"What happened to my guy?"

Joel shrugged. "Nothing to do with me."

"Yet you're driving his car."

Joel said nothing.

"If I find out you had something to do with Ruben's disappearance, I'll fuck up your boy," Fineman said. "And if that doesn't get your attention, I'll come for your daughter, and then your wife, and then your mother."

Joel swallowed.

"You're insured. Your boat's insured," Fineman said. "You're worth more dead than alive, but your family, they aren't worth shit."

"What about you?" Joel asked. "You disappear and half the baymen in Montauk are debt free."

The loan shark smiled, a great white grin. "Well, that isn't going to happen."

Fineman pulled a ledger from his desk drawer, flipped it open, and made a mark. As he opened the safe next to his desk to put away the payment, he said, "Your father was a legend. He could find fish in a desert. You couldn't find them in an aquarium."

Remora's death had been self-defense, and until that moment Joel wasn't sure about his plan to eliminate his debt by framing the dead man for Fineman's murder. Now, though, he went ahead with it. He drew Remora's semi-automatic pistol from the small of his back and squeezed the trigger three times, hitting Fineman twice in the arm and once in the chest.

He had touched nothing in the house, and before he did, he pulled on a pair of latex gloves, taken from the same box as the pair he'd worn while driving the Equinox. He retrieved his envelope and took Fineman's ledger, filled a plastic trash bag with nearly half a million dollars from the loan shark's safe. He carried it out to the car and stuffed it into a roller bag he'd purchased earlier that day. Then he drove off, confident no one could have heard the shots.

He drove the Equinox to Long Island MacArthur Airport, left it in long-term parking, and dragged the roller bag behind him to the MTA's Long Island Railroad station, took the train to Montauk, where he'd left his F-250. He returned to the *Alexa II*, parked, and rolled the bag of money into the Sand Bar moments before last call. The place was deserted.

He paid off his tab and asked for a bottle of Jim Beam.

Eddie grabbed an unopened bottle from the back bar. "I saw you down by the *Alexa II*. You going out tonight?"

"I have a charter."

"You know better," Eddie said, pulling the bottle back. "Alcohol and the open sea don't mix."

"They do tonight." Joel wrestled the bottle from the old man's hand.

"Whatever you have planned, Joel, don't do it," the bartender said. "There's a storm coming."

Joel knew all about the incoming storm. He was counting on it to provide cover for the last piece of his plan.

"Do me a favor," he said, swinging the roller bag up onto the bar. "You hold onto this, give it to Jennifer when the time is right."

"How will I know—?"

"You'll know."

"I'll do it, Joel," Eddie said, making the roller bag disappear beneath the counter. "Just like I did what I did for your mother all those years ago."

"What are you talking about?"

"Your father didn't save my life. In fact, I almost died because of his poor decisions, but if I'd told the truth to the insurance investigators, they never would have paid out your mother's claim."

Joel hesitated before asking, "What are you telling me?"

"There was no rogue wave that night. Your father was stinking drunk when he sank the *Alexa*. I'm lucky to be alive."

Joel released his grip on the bottle and slid a wad of cash across the bar. "Get your damn leg fixed."

Then he walked back to the *Alexa II*, made sure Remora Ramirez's body was secure in the hold, and cast off.

*

Dawn had crept over the horizon and he had deep-sixed Remora's semi-automatic pistol and both Remora's and Fineman's debt records by the time he passed the Vineyard and turned into the channel between Chappaquiddick Island and Nantucket Island to top off his fuel tank in Nantucket Harbor. As he was leaving port, he saw a storm-warning flag and ignored it.

He rounded Nantucket Island and pointed the *Alexa II* almost due south toward the edge of the continental shelf, the Atlantis canyon, and the open ocean beyond.

His radio crackled to life, and the caller identified himself as Karl Winestadt. "Where you at, Joel?"

"Outbound from Nantucket."

When Karl heard that, he urged Joel to turn back. "There's a storm brewing, and it's going to be a bad one."

"I'm taking out a charter."

"You don't do charters."

"I need the money," Joel said.

"In this weather?"

"I don't have a choice," Joel explained. "It's tonight or never."

He heard static in reply.

"Tell Jennifer I love her," Joel said, his hands on the wheel, "but tonight I'm trolling Atlantis."

Between his life insurance, his boat insurance, and the half million in cash he'd left with Eddie, his family would be well cared for. Joel switched off the radio and steered into the oncoming storm.

He was born a bayman and he would die a bayman, and this time there would be no survivor to fabricate stories of his heroics.

River of Dreams
Released August 1993

"No Man's Land"
"The Great Wall of China"
"Blonde Over Blue"
"A Minor Variation"
"Shades of Grey"
"All About Soul"
"Lullaby (Goodnight, My Angel)"
"The River of Dreams"
"Two Thousand Years"
"Famous Last Words"

All songs by Billy Joel.

No Man's Land
by James D.F. Hannah

Barry washes the night down with a half-bottle of bourbon to balance out the cocaine, and he's dead asleep when two guys with necks like tree stumps knock the front door off its hinges. They find him in his bedroom and throw a pillowcase over his head, which rouses him to a state adjacent to consciousness.

"He don't look like no king to me," one says.

"At least he's wearing underwear," the other one says.

Barry instinctively tries to fight, but there's one of him and two of them. They meet his efforts with a blow to the base of his skull, and he's pulled under to a warm and comforting darkness.

*

Barry wakes with his face flush to plush cream-colored carpeting. A second later, he's kicked in the gut so hard his stomach grinds against his spine.

"Again." A man's voice. "Get his balls."

The kicker obliges. Waves of white-hot pain wash over him, and he empties the contents of his stomach—bourbon, medium-rare steak, baked potato—onto the carpet.

"Jesus Christ, Vinnie, you know what I paid a square foot for that?" A woman's voice now. Through nausea and the bite of acid at the back of his throat, Barry I.D.s it as Nora Anderson. He notes her concern for the carpet and not his family jewels.

Shadows shift and shapes sharpen with a few blinks. Nora, enveloped in a pink robe, orbits a thick-chested guy in a blue suit who pours a drink from a well stocked bar.

Barry guesses this is Nora Anderson's living room. High-dollar Long Island style, fake Grecian statuettes, paintings by artists whose names she can't pronounce, overpriced furniture arranged around a glass coffee table. A girl sobs in a chair. Honey-colored locks hide her face as she whines like kittens in a sack dangled over a river. Alicia Anderson, Nora's sixteen-year-old daughter.

Barry hears a groaning behind him. Twists around to see Scott Hauerback, an agent at Barry's office, a rising star in Long Island real estate. Except Hauerback's once impeccable features are now most definitely peccable. His face resembles mashed potatoes—if mashed potatoes could bleed—and he's buck-ass naked. Barry self-consciously tugs at his own white briefs, making sure everything's covered and tucked away.

The man in the blue suit sips his bourbon and pulls a chair around to face Barry and Hauerback.

The man's about Barry's age. The suit's expensive, and the shine on his black Gucci loafers is bright enough to shave by. He unbuttons his jacket and melts into the back of the chair.

"So you're the Real Estate King of Long Island," he says.

*

You see Barry Willard's face coming out of the ground like dandelions on "For Sale" signs all across the island, almost as many of them as there are Clinton/Gore placards. Ubiquitous at bus stops all the way out to Riverhead. His slogan is "Let me get you home!" His game-show-host visage is comfortable yet distant. The photo was taken after he got his teeth capped, before his hair thinned and he had to color the gray.

"Named Long Island's Real Estate King SIX YEARS STRAIGHT!" the yard signs announce.

Thing is, those six years were a long time ago.

*

The man rattles the ice cubes in his now-empty glass. Another man takes the glass, refills it, returns it.

Nora paces, pausing every few seconds to look at the man Barry guesses must be Vinnie. The look on her face is the exasperation of a wife at her husband.

Barry says, "You the ex?"

"I'm the husband," Vinnie says.

Another Nora pause. "We're getting a fucking divorce, Vinnie!"

"I'm not talkin' about that," he says, not looking at her. "Right now, I'm talkin' to Mr. Real Estate King here."

"His name's Barry," Nora says.

You're not helping, Barry thinks.

Hauerback moans, and that draws a shattering wail from Alicia. Barry grits his teeth at the sound—a mistake, because he feels something shatter in his mouth. He spits an actual shard of enamel onto the carpet, not a porcelain cap. Goddammit.

"Let 'em go, Vinnie," Nora says. "They didn't do nothin'."

Vinnie shakes his head. "I know exactly what these assholes did." Vinnie's nostrils flare, and Barry imagines steam blowing out like the bull in a Bugs Bunny cartoon. He sips his drink, disgust settling into his face. "I can't act like it's nothin'."

*

They call Barry the Real Estate King of Long Island, but what's it been since his last decent close? Six months? Eight? Long enough, he's getting looks from the other agents. Not sympathy, because that doesn't exist at Hooper Realty. More like when dogs realize a weakness in the pack. Incisors bared, ready for the smell of blood.

Except at Hooper Realty it's Drakkar Noir and "Any luck out there, old man?" Mostly the razzing comes from Hauerback. Twenty-six years old, features chiseled from stone, hundred-dollar haircut gelled into place. He's been the top seller for the past year. Just bought himself a Beemer. Used, but a late model. The ride of a man on the rise.

Hauerback marks more and bigger sales on the board in the office. Every time he writes one up, he walks past Barry and says, "That's how you do it, old man."

*

At the bar and grill where they gather for lunch, Barry's two scotches in while the other agents nurse the same beers for the entire meal. Hauerback's there, but he doesn't drink, doesn't smoke, just sits there looking satisfied with himself.

On the TV, the news keeps talking about the chick in Massapequa who shot her boyfriend's wife over the summer. Barry wonders if there's a seventeen-year-old out there hot enough to let her fuck up your life.

He orders a third scotch as everyone else disperses back out into sunlight and the workday. Everyone except Barry and Hauerback. They trade silent stares across the table.

Barry knocks a half-inch of ash off his cigarette. "Got any game you're working?"

Hauerback shrugs, his muscles rippling beneath his suit jacket. "Pieces on the board." Sips a Clearly Canadian. "What about you, old man? You got anything going?"

"I got stuff happening," Barry says.

Hauerback pats down his jacket, removes a folded sheet of paper from an inside pocket. "All that stuff you got happening, any of it hot this afternoon, or can you make some space?"

Barry knows what the paper is: a lead slip. Information on a potential client is gold. You guard it like you'd guard your child. Maybe closer. If Hauerback's handing him a lead, Barry's got to ask himself why. Probably absolute shit, a waste of time.

But Barry's schedule is a goddamn wasteland, all he's *got* is time.

"Fill me in," he says.

*

The client's name is Nora Anderson, and she keeps Barry waiting twenty minutes outside the first showing. Barry's in his Park Avenue, buzzing off a fresh bump, when the Volvo pulls up across the street. Nora flashes tanned leg and short skirt as she gets out of the Swedish-made moneymobile. She fishes cigarettes from her purse, lights one. She's forties and looks it, but looks it good. Somebody wrote checks to keep her like this.

She scans the sidewalk. Thirty seconds, already impatient.

Barry wipes his nostrils, checks himself in the rearview before crossing the street.

"Mrs. Anderson," he says. "So glad—"

She exhales a plume of smoke into his face. "Been waiting on you."

Barry gives a perfunctory glance to his watch. "I believe our appointment was at two, right?"

"Shit happens." A long inhale and an up-and-down. "Where's the other guy?" Twin veins of smoke exit her nostrils. "He was nice looking."

*

The showing schedule for Nora Anderson focuses on small houses in old neighborhoods. Post-war developments with well manicured lawns and an American car in every driveway. The houses lack style and flash, and style and flash are obviously a thing for Nora Anderson.

"This all you got?" she says.

"This is the market," he says. "Low supply, high demand."

When they pull up to the next showing, Barry notices the face she makes. *Let's get this over with.*

He takes her by the wrist before her door's even open. "This ain't right for you," he says, using his neighborhood voice. Not the one he uses to sell a house, but the one he uses when he calls his mother. "I got somewhere else."

They drive to a five-bedroom in Westhampton. Sprawling front yard, green and even as pool-table felt. Been on the market for months and nothing but crickets, because who needs this much house, right?

Nora Anderson apparently does. Approval registers on her face for the first time that day. "Okay, now we're getting' somewhere, Mr. Willard."

"Please, call me Barry." He adds a smile and a wink. It's like a nearly forgotten muscle memory, this sensation. This is what it feels like to be the Real Estate King of Long Island.

On the way to the next house, Nora makes a call on her mobile phone, a brick from the bottom of her purse. Calls her daughter, tells her to grab a cab and meet them.

They're checking a six-bedroom all-brick when a young woman's voice calls, "Where is everyone?"

"In the back, honey," Nora yells. To Barry she says, "That's my Alicia."

Barry has to take a breath when Alicia comes into the backyard. She might be the most perfect thing he's ever seen. Long straight hair shimmering in the late-afternoon sun. Bottlecap nose, full cheeks, lips that draw into a perfect bow. Her oversized sweatshirt denotes a Catholic school. Backpack slung over her shoulder, a field-hockey stick in hand.

Nora wraps her arm around her daughter's shoulder. "My Alicia's already getting talked up for scholarships. You should see her kick ass out there."

Alicia rolls her eyes. "He doesn't want to hear that, Mom."

"Hey, I got a right to be proud of my kid." Curls her lip. "Your father was any kind of man, he'd be proud of you, too."

"Christ, Mom, I—"

A whack upside the back of her head. "Watch your mouth."

Alicia scowls and rubs where her mother struck her.

The air suddenly feels thick and tense, and Barry excuses himself. Nora says something to Alicia about how a pool would look here.

Barry finds a bathroom and knocks out two lines of coke onto the edge of the sink, stripping them straight and even across the marble. Rolls up a twenty from his wallet and inhales a line. Tendrils of electricity spiral through his synapses, snapping to life a million little pieces of himself. That initial line is always Barry's favorite. Like falling in love for the first time.

He doesn't hear the bathroom door open, doesn't notice Alicia watching him. When he does, he freezes.

She takes the rolled twenty from his hand, powers the second line of coke up her nose. She holds the sink edge, pushes her chest forward and her head back as the spasms of euphoria hit her. Goose pimples fly across her arms and her pupils turn to pinpricks as she drops her gaze onto Barry. She grabs his lapels and pulls him to her and kisses him.

Barry's lizard brain takes over, hard-wired from caveman times. Biological imperative. He puts his arms around her, holds her tight, like she could float away. She tastes like pineapple lip gloss.

Alicia pushes him off. Her smile—sly and knowing, a look of secret knowledge she'll never share—returns.

"Not bad," she says. "I've had better."

She turns and walks out of the bathroom, Barry left unsure if she was judging the coke or the kiss.

*

Barry drives Nora and Alicia back to Nora's car. Alicia slides into the Volvo's backseat, looking like a Lolita behind heart-shaped sunglasses and a paperback of *In Cold Blood*. Barry considers similarities shared between mother and daughter: the apple hasn't fallen far from the tree, and the tree is still mighty fine. He also considers the leanness of Nora Anderson's calves and the sleekness of her thighs, and the glories and hallelujahs to which they surely lead.

"I think you might have yourself a sale with that last house," Nora says.

"Let me buy you a drink tonight," Barry says. "To celebrate."

*

They meet at a bar Barry knows well enough the piano player gives him a wave as they enter. Midway through her second gin and tonic, Nora mentions her ex, a prick named Vincent Anderson, who owns Anderson Shipping. Barry's seen the eighteen-wheelers on the LIE. This explains the Volvo, the perfect tits, the kid in a pricey private school.

"But after a while," she says on her third G&T, "the money wasn't worth it. I knew he'd fuck around on me, but he actually put her in an apartment. Paid her rent, Con Ed bills. I ain't standin' for that."

Nora's hand slips under the table, grabs Barry's knee. "What about you, Barry? You have your own sordid past?"

Barry looks into her gin-hazed eyes and laughs. "I don't spend much time thinking about the past. Selling real estate, you turn one person's yesterdays into someone else's tomorrows, so you got no time to worry about your own."

Nora's hand climbs higher up Barry's thigh.

"What about tonight?" she says. "Have you got time for that?"

*

Barry pays cash for a motel room. When the door is closed and locked and Nora's stepped out of her skirt suit, he sees she's wearing actual garters and stockings, like someone from a 1950s movie, like Marilyn Monroe or Jayne Mansfield.

*

Later, when Barry drops Nora back at her front door and drives off, he notices the black BMW.

Behind the wheel, a guy who looks like Hauerback.

Next to the guy who looks like Hauerback, a girl who looks like Alicia Anderson.

Barry flips a vicious U-turn. There's a chorus of horns and single-fingered salutes from the passing traffic, but he ignores them, his focus on the Beemer.

It's parked across the street from Nora Anderson's home, and Barry finds a spot several car lengths behind it. Far enough back they won't notice him, close enough to see Hauerback take Alicia Anderson's face into his hands and kiss her.

Alicia's still dressed in her school uniform when she comes out of the car. The next generation of her mother's firm, tanned legs pumping her through traffic and across the street. She stops at the sidewalk to look back at Hauerback with the blind adoration you only offer once in your life.

Barry can't do anything but laugh. "Sneaky little sonofabitch," he says.

What Barry doesn't notice is the Caddy, or the two gigantic men inside it. Watching him watching Hauerback.

*

Vinnie sets his glass aside. "The name Vincent Andretti mean anything to you?"

It does. Because you do business on Long Island, you do business with the Andrettis. Shipments on the waterfront? The Andrettis get a piece. Run a card game? You pay the Andretti family. Need permits for an addition, dig a pool, put up a tree house for your kid? Yeah, the Andrettis. The Andretti family gets a cut of more Long Island business than Uncle Sam. Difference is, Uncle Sam won't carve you up and bury you in four different locations if you jerk him around.

For Uncle Vinnie, though, that is the very cornerstone of his business model.

Vinnie leans forward, rests his forearms on his knees. "Now let's talk about you fuckin' my wife."

A sharp laugh from Nora. She's made herself a gin and tonic, drinking it from her position at the bar. Her robe parts, and Barry can see that she's naked underneath.

"You mind?" Vinnie says. "We're havin' a conversation here."

"Sure, sure," she says. Folds her arms across her chest. "You boys go right on. Talk about Barry and me. Can't wait to hear."

Creases furrow Vinnie's forehead. He looks back to Nora. Wearing a smile like a homecoming crown.

"Ask him about the motel," she says.

Barry thinking, *Just fucking kill me now.*

*

The motel is where chemistry and biology collide, and it's a ten-car pile-up, because Barry's doing so much coke nothing works like it should. His junk lies there, shriveled up like an earthworm on the sidewalk, drying out in the sun, disinterested in the entire process.

There's uncomfortable silence and cigarette smoking, and he tells her this has never happened before. She doesn't even pretend to believe him, and all she offers is a curt goodbye when he takes her home.

*

Vinnie stares at Barry like he's an alien species. "So you and Nora didn't fuck?"

"We did not," Barry says.

"What's your problem? My wife not hot enough for you?"

Alicia retches loudly. "Daddy, this is so gross!" Her first actual words, pushed through a picket fence of tears.

Vinnie checks over his shoulder. "Little girl, you and me will have a conversation once all this is done."

"But I *love* him," she says.

Vinnie throws himself out of the chair and storms in his daughter's direction. He's not a big man, but he becomes huge in his movement. She balls herself up tighter and smaller into the chair.

Nora swoops from the bar and steps between them. Alicia makes such a wail, Barry has hope for a second—maybe the cops are coming—before he realizes what he hears are the mournful cries of a teenager, not sirens.

"Barry?" Hauerback whispers. His eyes, swollen and purple, open into the tiniest of slits. His muscled physique is a Pollack painting, varying shades of bruises and dried blood.

Barry can't muster pity here. "You fucking moron." Contempt drips in every syllable. "You couldn't find a piece of underaged ass *not* tied to the Mob?"

That's when it hits Barry why Hauerback gave him a client who was obviously money.

To Hauerback, Barry's nothing but a washed-up old man, someone who'll keep Nora busy with shitty properties while Hauerback bangs the daughter.

Barry stretches out, pushes himself to his feet. Body screaming, stomach swimming, world spinning—*hello, concussion*—he presses his soles hard into Nora's expensive carpet, solidifying his stance.

"Hey!" he says. His voice reverberates like a gunshot, but it gets everyone's attention and, more importantly, shuts them the fuck up.

Vinnie glares at him. "Can I fucking help you?"

"Yeah," Barry says. "You gonna kill us or what?"

"Why? You got somewhere to be?"

"Maybe I have appointments in the morning."

Vinnie laughs with an edge of surprise. It's what Barry knows is the next-to-last sound some guys ever hear, just before the gunshot that sprays their gray matter onto a wall. He tells one of his goons to take Nora and Alicia upstairs. Alicia opens up a fresh round of screams and pounds at the goon with small fists, which is like trying to chop down a tree with a butter knife. The goon hoists the girl over his shoulder, carries her out of the room. Nora follows close behind, cursing Vinnie with every step. The voices dissipate into the recesses of the house. The silence left in their wake becomes more apparent.

Vinnie walks over to Barry, lays a hand on his shoulder. Casual. Two guys talking.

Barry swallows hard and struggles to keep his legs from collapsing.

"She don't understand, is the problem," Vinnie says. "I got a lot of stress, and sometimes I gotta take pressure off that valve."

"I don't think she's real concerned with your ... valves," Barry says. "I'd say she just doesn't want to be married anymore."

"The fuck that got to do with anything? Judge comes along, writes his name on a piece of paper? That don't mean nothin'. We're still married in the eyes of God."

"The eyes of God are the least of my worries right now, Mr. Andretti."

"Vinnie." He sighs, shakes his head. "You have put me in a position, Barry. People talk. I can't have guys mouthing off about this shit."

"I assure you, Vinnie, you let me walk out of here, you ain't never gonna hear my name again. Your ex—"

"She ain't my ex."

"It might be best if you accept she's gonna *be* your ex," Barry says. "That way, you both go on with your lives. You should find yourself someone who makes you happy."

An exotic dancer, Barry thinks. *Diamond or Krystal or Amethyst. Have fun, let her work out her daddy issues.*

Hauerback pushes himself upright and says, "Vinnie, please, I—"

"Shut your mouth, asshole," Vinnie says. His face flushes red. "I'm Mr. Andretti to you."

Hauerback collapses back onto the floor.

Vinnie goes to the couch where Alicia's school equipment is. He picks up the field-hockey stick. Balances it, judging it.

"You doing coke?" Vinnie says to Barry.

"Yeah."

"Fucks up your dick." Pause. "You sure you didn't fuck my wife?"

"I swear," Barry says. *Not for lack of effort.*

"Fine, then. But you gotta know, this ain't a thing you just walk out of. You gotta have some skin in the game."

Vinnie hands Barry the stick. Barry feels the weight of it in his hand, and he understands.

"Get yourself a little dirty, then maybe we can talk some business," Vinnie says. He shrugs and sips his bourbon. "I got properties. I need a guy I can trust."

Hauerback's coiled on the floor, shaking like he's freezing. Barry thinks it must be shock.

It'll be the merciful thing. Quicker than Vinnie's goons.

The casualness of the thought stuns him.

Jesus Christ, are you really going to do this?

But what choice does he have? Hauerback is *not* walking out of here. If Barry does it, at least it'll be quick.

He grips the stick like a samurai sword and brings it up over his head.

Swing it hard, one fast blow, and it'll be done.

A long breath. Hauerback, eyes looking up like a puppy's, tears streaming down his cheeks.

Barry has never really liked Hauerback. His sales went down the day Hauerback started. With him gone, Barry can get back on his throne.

Especially with Vinnie in his corner.

"We work together," Vinnie says, at the bar, adding fresh ice to his glass, reading Barry's mind, "you gotta get off the coke."

Barry's already decided he's never doing coke again. Well, at the very least, he'll cut way back.

He hopes Vinnie never finds out about Alicia doing that line with him. Or the kiss.

One.

Hauerback's teeth chatter, his eyes roll back, nothing but white in the narrow slits.

Two.

The sound of bourbon being poured. "That's the thing about business," Vinnie says. "You gotta get your hands dirty."

Barry tells himself there's no turning back now. No reversals, no return trip. Welcome to No Man's Land.

Three.

This is what it takes to be the king, he tells himself, bringing the stick down hard onto Hauerback's skull.

Christ, but what this'll do to the carpet.

Acknowledgments

My thanks to the authors who enthusiastically contributed stories, to Jay Hartman and K.D. Sullivan at Untreed Reads for shepherding *Only the Good Die Young* through the publication process ... and, most of all, to the incomparable Billy Joel, whose music and lyrics inspired this book.

About the Contributors

MICHAEL BRACKEN has written several books, including the private eye novel *All White Girls*, but he's better known as the author of more than thirteen hundred short stories published in *Alfred Hitchcock's Mystery Magazine, Ellery Queen's Mystery Magazine, Espionage, Mike Shayne Mystery Magazine, The Best American Mystery Stories*, and many other anthologies and periodicals. He is the editor of *Black Cat Mystery Magazine*, the Anthony Award finalist *The Eyes of Texas: Private Eyes from the Panhandle to the Piney Woods*, and other anthologies. He lives, writes, and edits in Texas. *www.CrimeFictionWriter.com*

JEFF COHEN, who also writes as E.J. Copperman, has published twenty-six crime novels (so far!); the latest is *Inherit the Shoes*, first in the Jersey Girl Legal Mystery series. For about fifteen minutes many years ago, he was a newspaper reporter, and he continues to write for magazines and newspapers while teaching at Drexel University. He's probably writing another novel even as you read this. *www.ejcopperman.com*

DAVID DEAN is a retired New Jersey chief of police and once served as a paratrooper with the 82nd Airborne Division. His short stories have been nominated for the Shamus, Barry, and Derringer awards, he won the EQMM Readers Award in 2007 (for "Ibrahim's Eyes") and in 2019 (for "The Duelist"), and he was an Edgar finalist in 2011 (for "Tomorrow's Dead"). His three novels — *The Thirteenth Child, Starvation Cay*, and *The Purple Robe* — are available on Amazon.

JOHN M. FLOYD's work has appeared in more than three hundred different publications, including AHMM, EQMM, *The Strand Magazine, The Saturday Evening Post*, and three editions of *The Best American Mystery Stories*. A former Air Force captain and IBM systems engineer, he is also an Edgar finalist, a four-time Derringer Award winner, a 2018 recipient of the Edward D. Hoch Memorial Golden Derringer Award for Lifetime Achievement, and the author of nine books. *johnmfloyd.com*

BARB GOFFMAN loves writing, reading, air conditioning, and her dog, not necessarily in that order. She's won the Agatha, Macavity, and Silver Falchion awards for her short stories, and she's been a finalist twenty-seven times for national mystery short-story awards, including the Anthony and Derringer. Her book *Don't Get Mad, Get Even* won the Silver Falchion for the best collection of 2013. Her stories have also appeared in AHMM, EQMM, BCMM and a number of anthologies, including *Crime Travel*, a time-travel crime anthology she edited. Barb lives in Winchester, Virginia, and works as a freelance editor and proofreader. *www.barbgoffman.com*

JAMES D.F. HANNAH is the author of the Henry Malone novels; *Behind the Wall of Sleep* won the Private Eye Writers of America's Shamus Award for Best Paperback Original in 2019. His short fiction has appeared in *A Rock and a Hard Place, Crossed Genres, Shotgun Honey, The Anthology of Appalachian Writers,* and *Trouble No More: Crime Fiction Inspired by the Allman Brothers.* Born in West Virginia and raised in Kentucky, he was an award-winning journalist before moving into governmental public relations. *www.jamesdfhannah.com*

RICHARD HELMS, a retired forensic psychologist and college professor, has been a Derringer Award finalist eight times (with two wins), a Shamus finalist six times, an International Thriller Writers Thriller Award finalist twice (with a win in 2011), and a Macavity finalist. His story "See Humble and Die" was reprinted in *The Best American Mystery Stories 2020,* his novel *Paid in Spades* won the Killer Nashville Silver Falchion Award in 2020, and his twentieth novel, *Brittle Karma*, was published in November 2020 by Black Arch Books. He lives in Charlotte, NC, with his wife Elaine. *www.richardhelms.net*

ROBERT LOPRESTI is a retired librarian who lives in the Pacific Northwest. His most recent novel, *Greenfellas*, is a comic tale of the Mafia trying to save the environment. His seventy-plus short stories have won the Derringer and Black Orchid Novella awards, been a finalist for the Anthony, and been reprinted in *The Best American*

Mystery Stories. He is the current president of the Short Mystery Fiction Society. *roblopresti.com*

JENNY MILCHMAN is the author of five novels of psychological suspense (most recently *The Second Mother*), has won the Mary Higgins Clark and Silver Falchion awards, and has been a finalist for the Macavity and Anthony awards. Her books have been chosen four times for *Indie Next Picks* and included on various year's-best lists. Co-chair of the debut authors program for the ITW and a member of the Sisters in Crime Speakers Bureau, she lives in the mountains of New York State with her family. *jennymilchman.com*

TERRIE FARLEY MORAN is the author of the beachside Read 'Em and Eat cozy mystery series and the co-author of Laura Childs' New Orleans scrapbooking mystery series. Her short stories have appeared in EQMM, AHMM, *Mystery Weekly*, and numerous anthologies. Her most recent novel, the latest in the long-running Jessica Fletcher series, is *Murder She Wrote: Killing in a Koi Pond*. She is a recipient of both the Agatha and the Derringer awards. *www.terriefarleymoran.com*

RICHIE NARVAEZ is the author of the award-winning collection *Roachkiller and Other Stories* and the thriller *Hipster Death Rattle*. His most recent novel is the historical YA mystery *Holly Hernandez and the Death of Disco*, and his newest book is the short-story collection *Noiryorican*. He lives in the Bronx. *richienarvaez.com*

JOSH PACHTER is a writer, editor, and translator, and the 2020 recipient of the Short Mystery Fiction Society's Edward D. Hoch Memorial Golden Derringer Award for Lifetime Achievement. Almost a hundred of his short crime stories have appeared in EQMM, AHMM, and many other places. He is the editor of *The Great Filling Station Holdup: Crime Fiction Inspired by the Songs of Jimmy Buffett* (Down and Out Books, 2021), *The Beat of Black Wings: Crime Fiction Inspired by the Songs of Joni Mitchell* (Untreed Reads, 2020), *The Misadventures of Nero Wolfe* (Mysterious Press, 2020), and

other anthologies, and his translations of stories by Dutch and Flemish crime writers appear regularly in EQMM.
www.joshpachter.com

CPSIA information can be obtained
at www.ICGtesting.com
Printed in the USA
BVHW040428070223
658034BV00002B/18

9 781953 601438